7/2019

BOWEN ISLAND LIBRARY
3 0947 0005 6063 7

D1006060

Bowen Island Public Library

WILLIAM WENTON
AND THE
LOST CITY

SOLVE THE PUZZLES! CRACK THE CODES!

William Wenton and the Impossible Puzzle
William Wenton and the Secret Portal
William Wenton and the Lost City

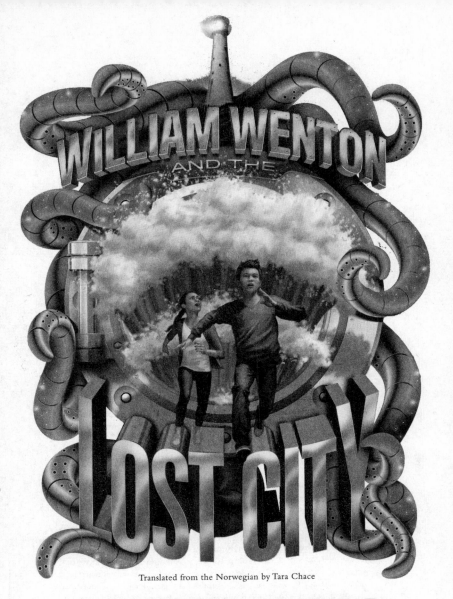

WILLIAM WENTON
AND THE
LOST CITY

Translated from the Norwegian by Tara Chace

BOBBIE PEERS

Aladdin
New York   London   Toronto   Sydney   New Delhi

This book is a work of fiction. Any references to historical events, real people, or real places are used fictitiously. Other names, characters, places, and events are products of the author's imagination, and any resemblance to actual events or places or persons, living or dead, is entirely coincidental.

ALADDIN

An imprint of Simon & Schuster Children's Publishing Division
1230 Avenue of the Americas, New York, New York 10020
First Aladdin hardcover edition July 2019
Text copyright © 2017 by Bobbie Peers
English language translation copyright © 2019 by Tara F. Chace
Originally published in Norway in 2017 as *Orbulateragenten* by H. Aschehoug & Co. (W. Nygaard), Oslo
Published by arrangement with Salomosson Agency
Jacket illustration of tentacles, lighthouse copyright © 2019 by Luke Lucas
Jacket illustration of boy, girl copyright © 2019 by Eric Deschamps
All rights reserved, including the right of reproduction in whole or in part in any form.
ALADDIN and related logo are registered trademarks of Simon & Schuster, Inc.
For information about special discounts for bulk purchases, please contact Simon & Schuster
Special Sales at 1-866-506-1949 or business@simonandschuster.com.
The Simon & Schuster Speakers Bureau can bring authors to your live event.
For more information or to book an event, contact the Simon & Schuster Speakers Bureau
at 1-866-248-3049 or visit our website at www.simonspeakers.com.
Cover designed by Heather Palisi
The text of this book was set in Bembo.
Manufactured in the United States of America 0619 FFG
2 4 6 8 10 9 7 5 3 1
Library of Congress Cataloging-in-Publication Data
Names: Peers, Bobbie, author. | Chace, Tara, translator.
Title: William Wenton and the lost city / by Bobbie Peers ;
translated from the Norwegian by Tara Chace.
Other titles: Orbulateragenten. English
Description: First Aladdin hardcover edition. | New York : Aladdin, 2019. |
Series: William Wenton ; 3 | "Originally published in Norway by H. Aschehoug & Co
as Orbulateragenten." | Summary: "William Wenton is a code-breaking genius, but when his secret
talent is suddenly revealed, he has to face the danger that has been lurking around him for years
in the third book in the William Wenton series"— Provided by publisher.
Identifiers: LCCN 2018057767 (print) | LCCN 2018060167 (eBook) |
ISBN 9781481478335 (eBook) | ISBN 9781481478311 (hc)
Subjects: | CYAC: Ciphers—Fiction. | Puzzles—Fiction. | Mystery and detective stories. |
Science fiction. | BISAC: JUVENILE FICTION / Mysteries & Detective Stories. | JUVENILE
FICTION / Humorous Stories. | JUVENILE FICTION / Fantasy & Magic.
Classification: LCC PZ7.1.P4397 (eBook) | LCC PZ7.1.P4397 Wie 2019 (print) | DDC [Fic]—dc23
LC record available at https://lccn.loc.gov/2018057767

To Michelle,
had it not been for you, this book
would never have been!

BIG BEN,
LONDON

The world-renowned clock tower loomed darkly over the grand buildings. Gray moonlight was reflected in the clock face. The gigantic hands said three thirty. London was quiet now, so quiet that from down on the street you could almost hear the clockwork inside the tower way up above. But in the nighttime darkness the ticking was soon replaced by something else.

Footsteps.

The dim light of a streetlamp revealed the shadow of a person growing in time with the footsteps. At last a tall figure came into view and stopped in front of the fence surrounding Big Ben.

It was a man wearing a broad-brimmed hat and a long overcoat. He glanced up at the clock face. For a moment he stood completely still, like a statue on the dark street. Then, in one quick bound, he leaped the fence and strode over to the wall of the clock tower. He fumbled around in his pockets until he finally found what he was looking for: a small metal door no bigger than a matchbox. He ran a pale hand over the textured limestone wall, and as if the stone were magnetic, he secured the little metal door to it. With a series of clicks and mechanical movements, the metal door began to grow, becoming larger and larger until it was the size of a regular door.

The man glanced around warily before opening the door, stepping inside, and closing it behind him.

A short time later, the door opened once again, and the man emerged, holding something in his hands. It looked heavy and was wrapped in a dirty cloth.

He shut the door behind him. It shrank, and the man plucked it back off the wall. He returned it to his pocket and looked around before leaping back over the fence and vanishing into the darkness.

The sound of his footsteps faded away, and then there was complete silence. It was even quieter than before.

Big Ben had stopped.

In a secret control center at the Institute for Post-Human Research in England, a red alarm light started flashing. Beneath the light was a small label that said BIG BEN,

LONDON. A frightened technician looked up. He swallowed his coffee the wrong way and broke into a violent coughing fit, but his eyes remained transfixed by the flashing light the entire time.

"Call Goffman," he said, his voice quavering. "Now!"

1

"William . . . ," a voice said.

William rolled over and pulled his pillow over his head.

"William . . . ," the voice said again. "You have to get up."

"Just a couple minutes," William grunted. "Just a couple more minutes."

"NOW, WILLIAM!"

He sat up and looked around. He had bed head, and his eyelids felt heavy. He glanced at the laptop on his nightstand. His grandfather's face smiled back at him from the screen.

"I'll be in trouble with your mother if I don't get you up on time," his grandfather said. "So you're going to have to get up no matter how tired you are."

"I know, I know . . . ," William mumbled, swinging his feet out of bed. The floor was cold, and he wanted to hide under his covers again. At the moment he thought his grandfather was lucky he was a computer program—he didn't have to wake up in the morning.

"You need to be out the door in nineteen minutes," his grandfather said.

William scrambled out of bed and found his clothes.

With both his mother and father at work, his grandfather was responsible for making sure William made it to school on time. Now that his father was able to get around without a wheelchair, thanks to the exoskeleton he had received from the Institute, he was working at the local museum. It was the same museum where William had cracked the world's most difficult code a little over a year ago, and had his life turned upside down.

"How many days are left now?" William asked, pulling his sweater on over his head.

It had become a ritual they performed every morning. William knew the answer but liked to hear his grandfather say it anyway. He could hardly wait to get back to the Institute.

"Eleven days," his grandfather said, smiling. "And you have fifteen minutes until your bus leaves. You should unplug me."

William walked over to the laptop.

"Have a good day," his grandfather said with a wink. "And keep out of trouble."

"You too," William said, and waved. He turned off the computer and pulled out the thumb drive.

Then he walked over to his grandfather's old desk and carefully placed the thumb drive in the drawer before taking out a small key and locking it.

Ten minutes later, William was running down the driveway in front of his house. He'd buttered a slice of bread at the last minute, and as he turned onto the sidewalk, he took a big bite, then stopped abruptly. A man wearing a red uniform and a hat that was pulled down so far the visor hid his face was standing in front of him. He held a small gray package in his hands.

"William?" he said.

William hesitated.

"William Wenton?" the man repeated, taking a step closer. He clicked as he walked. William glanced down at the man's shoes. They were white and black. Was he wearing tap shoes?

William looked around. There was an old, dented red mail truck parked in the street, but otherwise it was completely deserted.

"I have a very important express delivery for William Wenton," the man said. "Is that you?"

William forced himself to swallow the buttered bread in his mouth. "Yes," he eventually replied.

"Do you have some ID?" the mailman said.

"Uh." William thrust his hand into his pocket and pulled out his bus pass.

"You don't have one with a picture on it?"

"It says my name right there," William said, pointing.

The mailman muttered something to himself as he carefully tucked the package under his arm and inspected the bus pass.

"All right," he said after a moment, taking a step back. "I believe you. It's an honor to finally meet you, young Master Wenton." He bowed and tapped his shoes against the sidewalk a couple of times. Then he handed back the bus pass and held out the package. "Here you go."

William took it and was surprised at how heavy it was.

"What is it?" he asked, shaking the package a little.

"Careful," the mailman said. "It's supposed to be handled with care. And you need to be alone when you open it."

"Alone?"

William tried to look into the mailman's eyes, but the shadow from his visor still covered his face.

"Completely alone. This is not a dance for two."

William suddenly heard his bus down the street.

"I have to go," he said, and set out at a run for the bus stop.

"Handle with care!" he heard the man yell after him.

William reached the bus stop just as the bus doors slid open. As he climbed on, he turned and looked back toward his driveway. The mailman was still standing there staring at him, but by the time William found himself a seat and the bus drove past his house, the mysterious man was gone.

2

Mr. Humburger paced back and forth in front of the board.

"And when you hear the fire alarm . . ." He paused and eyed his students sternly. "Then you all stand up, nicely and orderly, and walk out the door in a line."

William sat in his seat and tried to concentrate on what his teacher was saying. But it was hard, since his thoughts were being constantly drawn to the strange package in his backpack.

"Then we'll gather by class out in the schoolyard and wait quietly for the fire department to arrive," Mr. Humburger continued.

There was going to be a fire drill. The students generally looked forward to these, because it meant a break from schoolwork. And today's would be extra exciting: The fire department was actually supposed to come.

Mr. Humburger glanced up at the clock on the wall.

As the second hand hit twelve, an alarm out in the hallway started wailing. Chairs scraped as the whole class stood up at the same time.

"No panic," Mr. Humburger urged as he directed the students with both arms.

William knew the teachers competed to see who could get their class outside first.

Mr. Humburger jogged over to the door and waved to his students. "Line up, everyone. Leave your backpacks here. We're coming back."

William leaned over and carefully lifted the package out of his backpack and hid it under his sweater. This fire drill suited him perfectly. No one would notice if he snuck off. He had to find out what the strange man had given him.

"Everyone, march in time with the beat," Mr. Humburger yelled. Then he placed a whistle in his mouth and started blowing the beat at the top of his lungs as he led the way out the door.

The whole class followed, marching down the hallway like a meager little parade for Norway's national holiday, the Seventeenth of May. As William's class moved along, other students started streaming out of their classrooms as well, and Mr. Humburger had to hurry. He sped up his whistling, and the marching students tried to keep pace.

William scanned the hallway. Now was his chance to

hide. The door to the teachers' lounge stood open, and the room was deserted. Glancing around quickly, he ducked out of line and snuck inside. Mr. Humburger's whistle faded into the distance.

William waited until it was totally quiet in the hallway. Then he walked over to the window and peered out. Three fire trucks drove onto the school grounds. Mr. Humburger was trying to direct them, but the drivers ignored him and parked in a completely different location.

Breathing a sigh of relief, William sat down on the sofa. He placed the package on the coffee table in front of him and stared at it for a few seconds.

Scooting to the edge of the cushion, William untied the twine and started carefully removing the thick gray paper. He remembered what the mailman had said: The package had to be handled with care.

His heart beat faster. There were multiple layers of paper, but slowly something began to come into view.

A metal pyramid.

It was covered with strange geometric figures that pulsed with white light.

The familiar vibrations began right away. They started in his belly before continuing up his spine. In William's head the symbols on the pyramid began to come loose from the metal surface and hover in the air in front of him.

A code.

The pyramid was a code!

William quickly leaned back on the sofa, and the hovering symbols fell back into place. He wanted to solve it, but he was scared. The last time he'd solved a code without knowing what it did, he'd activated a portal in the Himalayas. William wasn't planning to make that mistake again. He had to talk to his grandfather before he did anything at all. He was about to wrap the pyramid back up when the door flew open, and Mr. Humburger stormed in.

"There you are!" he yelled. "We lost the lineup competition because of you. What are you doing in here, anyway?!" Then he spotted the pyramid. "And what is that?"

Before William had a chance to respond, Mr. Humburger snatched it from him.

"No, be careful . . . ," William protested.

The pyramid started emitting sparks, and Mr. Humburger screamed and dropped it back onto the coffee table.

"What's it doing?" he yelled, staggering backward. "Make it stop!"

He stumbled into the wall and remained frozen there.

The pyramid kept sparking as it vibrated its way across the table. William reached for it, but it fell onto the floor and kept going toward Mr. Humburger.

"What does it want?" Mr. Humburger yelled, pressing himself against the wall. "Why is it after me?"

"I don't think it's after anyone," William said, standing up.

The pyramid stopped vibrating and lay at Mr. Humburger's feet.

Sweat was pouring down the man's face, and he was opening and closing his mouth like a goldfish.

"Don't touch it," William said, edging cautiously closer.

"There'll be consequences for this, William," Mr. Humburger snarled. "Is it finished?" He stretched his foot out and kicked the pyramid.

"No, wait," William said.

The pyramid emitted a deafening howl, and a geyser of sparks shot out of it.

Mr. Humburger was in a complete panic now. He jumped over the pyramid, sprinted to the window, and yanked it open. He stuck his head out and yelled at the top of his lungs: "ALARM, ALARM!"

Everyone who was standing down in the schoolyard looked up.

"THERE'S A FIRE . . . THERE'S A REAL FIRE UP HERE!"

A fireman holding a firehose turned and pointed the hose at the window.

Mr. Humburger gasped for breath and tried to yell again, but the effort and his panic had drained the air out of him. He settled for flailing his arms around wildly.

A powerful jet of water shot out of the firehose and hit Mr. Humburger in the chest with tremendous force. He was flung backward and landed on his back a little way from the window. William ran over and tried to help him up, but Mr. Humburger pushed him away and scrambled to his feet on his own.

"I have to get out," Mr. Humburger yelled, pulling off his drenched T-shirt. "I have to get to the roof."

"No, that's dangerous!" William yelled, but the man didn't pay any attention.

"I need to buy myself a little time. I've been practicing this," he said; then he pressed his wet T-shirt to his face and ran out into the hallway.

William stood there. He turned and looked at the pyramid, which now sat completely still on the floor.

When William walked out into the schoolyard, everyone was staring up at the building he had just exited. He had hidden the pyramid under his sweater and was holding his hands over it protectively to hide the angular bulge. He glanced up at the roof and spotted Mr. Humburger, who was standing up there waving both arms. He had taken off his pants and tied them around his head. His pale white body gleamed in the sun.

The firemen were holding the sides of something that looked like an enormous trampoline. They ran over to the school building and stopped right under where Mr. Humburger was standing.

"THE ONLY WAY IS DOWN," Mr. Humburger yelled.

"No, wait!" one of the firemen shouted as another fireman stepped out of the main entrance and shook his head. "There's no fire. It's a false alarm."

But Mr. Humburger wasn't listening. He positioned himself right on the edge of the roof and stretched both arms up into the air like a competitive diver.

And then in an elegant motion, he launched himself off in a perfect swan dive. A gasp ran through the crowd, which followed Mr. Humburger's journey down to the life net the firemen on the ground were holding out below him.

With a wet squish, Mr. Humburger landed belly first.

3

William sat in the backseat watching rows of buildings
glide by. It was raining. The car windows were fogged up, and
it made the world on the outside feel remote and insignifi-
cant.

"Can you believe the nerve of that teacher?" William's
mother grumbled, clenching the steering wheel so tightly
that her knuckles turned white.

"You need to shift up," William's father said, gesturing
at the gear shift.

"And that principal!" his mother hissed.

William and his parents had been at the principal's
office. There, Mr. Humburger made a production out of
blaming William for what had happened and demanded
that he be expelled immediately. The principal, as usual,

tiptoed around the subject. Something that made William's mother even more furious.

"We need to hurry," his father urged, glancing at his battery display, which showed how much charge remained for his exoskeleton. "I've only got eight percent left. And you need to change gears now."

"How can it be William's fault that that silly man did a swan dive off the roof in his underwear?" his mother continued, still in the same gear.

William looked at the backpack on the seat beside him. The package was in there. He could hardly wait to show his grandfather. If anyone would know what it was, it was him.

"They should fire him," his mother continued, turning the wheel hard to the side. The car veered into their driveway and came to a stop.

His mother undid her seat belt and was about to get out, but something held her back. She was staring at the house.

"William, were you the last one to leave this morning?" she finally asked.

"Yes," William said, looking up. "Why?"

"The front door's open."

William leaned forward. She was right. The front door was ajar.

"I definitely remember locking it," William said.

"And what's that?" his mother asked, pointing to the kitchen window.

William leaned even farther forward and squinted through the fogged-up windshield.

There was some kind of brown substance on the inside of the kitchen window.

"Up there, too," his mother said, pointing to the windows on the second floor. "It's the same in all the windows. What happened in there?"

"Let's find out." His father opened his car door and got out. "Wait here," he instructed, and then approached the house. His heavy exoskeleton clunked against the driveway.

William watched his father move toward the front door. Was his dad really planning to go in there? Alone?

"Alfred . . . ," his mom said, getting out of the car. "We should call the police."

His father ignored her, opening the door a bit more and walking in.

William followed his mother. They stopped just outside the door. They could hear William's father poking around inside. Then it grew quiet.

"I'm going to go in and check," William said. "Maybe his battery died, and he can't move."

"We'll go together," his mother said, pushing the door all the way open.

They stopped in the front hallway and stared.

The brown stuff they'd seen in the windows covered the entire floor and came up to his father's knees. It was sawdust or wood shavings—the entire house was covered in sawdust.

"Dad?" William whispered.

But his father didn't respond.

It seemed like the sawdust absorbed all the sound in the house. And William wasn't even sure if his voice was audible. He started down the hallway, wading through sawdust.

His father stood frozen, staring at something in the living room.

William stopped a few yards from him.

"Dad?" he said cautiously.

"In all my life I've never seen anything like this . . . ," his father whispered.

William walked over to stand beside him and peered into the room.

All their furniture was gone. Sawdust lay in deep drifts up against the windows, as if there'd been a snowstorm.

"What happened?" William asked.

"Don't know," his father said. He leaned over and picked up a fistful of sawdust, letting it sift between his fingers. "It kind of looks like all the furniture was pulped," he said thoughtfully.

"Pulped?" William said. "What does that mean?"

"Shredded, destroyed," his father replied. "It means that everything in here is gone. . . ."

Suddenly a terrible thought occurred to William.

"No . . . ," he said before turning and running to the stairs.

"Wait," his father called after him.

But William raced up the stairs, taking them three at a time. He rushed into his room and stopped.

This room looked just like every other room in the house. The floor was covered with a thick layer of sawdust. The bed, the chair, the bookshelf, and the big desk that used to belong to his grandfather were all gone. Everything was just wood shavings.

"No . . . no . . . no . . . ," William repeated as he waded over to where the desk had been.

He dropped to his knees and started digging through the sawdust. But in vain. His heart sank.

The desk was gone. . . .

And with it, the thumb drive with his grandfather on it.

William heard his father's voice behind him:

"We have to go. Now!"

The Wenton family sped down the highway.

It was too dangerous to contact the police, his mother had said. If someone could destroy their house, they were presumably also capable of coming back and doing worse things. The police were no match for that.

"The most important thing now is to get away and contact the Institute ASAP," his father said.

William was trembling, but he needed to think. If the thumb drive was really destroyed, did that mean his grandfather was gone?

"Don't worry about Grandpa," his father said, as if he'd read his mind. "All we need to do is activate the backup."

William took a breath.

"But to do that we need to get to the Institute. Relax,

William. Grandpa will be back again soon."

William sank into the seat. His father's words had helped him calm down, but he still had a shivery feeling. Taking care of the thumb drive had been his responsibility. His grandfather had trusted him, and now William felt like he had let him down.

He tried not to think about it. His thoughts turned back to what had happened at their house. Who in the world had destroyed everything in it? And why? He held on to his mysterious package even more tightly. He hadn't had a chance to tell his parents about it. But he had a terrible feeling that the package had something to do with all this.

While he sat there thinking, he noticed his eyelids getting heavier and heavier. A dancing mailman with no face grabbed him and chained his foot to the heavy pyramid. The only way William could free himself from the pyramid was by solving it. But he didn't have much time. It was a ticking bomb. Suddenly he was surrounded by half-naked Mr. Humburgers who were coming closer and closer, sneering malevolently. He took a step backward and suddenly realized he was standing by a cliff. A mechanical hand appeared out of nowhere and gave him the last final nudge, which was all it took. He fell.

William awoke with a start and looked around.

He was still in the backseat of the car, which was traveling at high speed. He didn't know how long he'd been asleep, but it must have been a while, because it was completely dark out now.

His parents were in the middle of a hushed conversation. And it didn't seem like they'd noticed that he was awake.

"... but why can't we just call them?" his mother asked.

"We'll wait until tomorrow," his father said. "I need time to think."

"Think about what?" his mother said, irritated. "Are we just going to drive around without any purpose? Besides, your battery is dead. You can't even get out of the car. We need to drive to the airport and get to the Institute. That's the safest place to be right now."

His father didn't answer, just sat there staring out into the darkness ahead of the car.

"Can we stop?" William said. "I have to pee."

His mother glanced at him in the rearview mirror.

"Do we have to?" his father asked.

William nodded.

"Okay, but be quick. We need to get as far away as possible," his father said.

"We've already come quite far," his mother said, and then looked out at the endless wheat fields around them stretching far off into the darkness.

She slowed down and pulled off to the side.

"Stay nearby," she instructed as William opened the door and got out.

He pulled his jacket closer around himself and strode out into the field. The cold air prickled in his nostrils. The sky was clear and full of stars.

The hum of the engine rumbled gently behind him as he walked, and soon he heard only the sound of the wind and the rustling of the wheat around him.

It suddenly felt like he was the only person on the planet. He looked up at the stars and wondered if Freddy was out there somewhere. Freddy had been a candidate at the Institute with William, but he had vanished through the Crypto Portal along with Abraham Talley. Were they together now? William couldn't imagine anything worse than being alone with Abraham. Abraham was the only one in the world, apart from himself, with luridium in his body. But unlike William, Abraham chose to use the powers the metal gave him to benefit himself. And now he'd traveled through the Crypto Portal to bring the luridium back to earth. William's eyes slid across the night sky. Before Abraham's assistant, Cornelia Strangler, had dissolved, she'd said that he would return, which was a frightening thought. Maybe what was happening now had something to do with Abraham.

William kept walking and noticed two stars hanging low over the treetops, twinkling more brightly than all the others.

"Not so far, William," his mother called from somewhere behind him.

He was out in the middle of the field now. He couldn't

quite shake the thought that there was some connection between the strange pyramid in his backpack and what had happened at their house.

He looked up. The two glowing stars above the treetops shone clear and bright. William was taken aback. Had they gotten bigger?

Now he could hear a rumbling from somewhere nearby.

The sound reminded him of a lawn mower. And it kept getting louder. He looked around. Everything was still deserted and dark. But those two stars had grown even brighter and bigger. It was as if they were getting closer.

Without taking his eyes off the stars, William walked backward through the wheat stalks.

They couldn't be stars. As they came closer, he realized they were two extremely bright lights. William backed away, faster and faster.

The lights stopped in the air and hung there.

William also stopped.

He didn't move a muscle.

He had only one thought in his head: *Please don't let it be Abraham Talley . . . please don't let it be Abraham Talley . . . please don't let—*

Suddenly the whole area was bathed in light.

William spun around and raced to the car, yanked open the door, and threw himself in.

"DRIVE!" he yelled.

5

William looked out the rear window at the lights coming after him.

"What is it?" his mother exclaimed.

"Just drive!" his father cried.

His mother stepped on the gas, and the car raced down the deserted road.

The engine whined, and blue smoke rose from the front tires. The smell of burning rubber filled the car. And along with the smell came a paralyzing fear.

Cornelia Strangler had almost killed William, and the smell of burned rubber had always followed her. But he knew it couldn't be her—she had destroyed herself in the Crypto Portal.

William had never seen his mother drive so fast. With clenched hands, she gripped the steering wheel as the car zoomed along the country road, while the lights followed them relentlessly. William held on as best he could and tried to see what exactly was behind them, but the lights blinded him. They were like two evil eyes.

They had left the wheat fields and were now surrounded on all sides by trees.

"In there!" his father shouted, pointing to a narrow dirt road.

"I don't know . . . ," his mother said skeptically.

"Turn!" his father insisted. "It's our only chance."

His mother spun the wheel hard, and the tires squealed as the car swerved off the paved roadway.

The lights following them abruptly stopped moving and hung in the air out on the main road.

"It stopped!" William cried.

Branches whipped the sides of the car as it raced down the narrow gravel track. The lights behind them grew smaller and smaller until they disappeared behind the trees that blocked out the moon. The car's headlights were the only source of illumination.

"How far should we go?" his mother asked. "We don't even know where this road leads."

She had her hands full keeping the car on the narrow road. Every now and then the wheels slid off into the ditch along the side, but each time she managed to maneuver the car back on track.

"There," his father called, pointing to something a little way ahead of them. "A road."

His mother turned the wheel, and they pulled out onto a wide, paved road. This one was lit with bright streetlights. After the dark journey through the woods, it was almost like driving out into the daylight.

"Did we do it? Did we get away?" his mother asked.

"I don't know," William said. "I hope so."

He got up onto his knees on the backseat and stared out the rear window. He hadn't seen even a glimpse of the lights since they'd turned onto the unpaved road.

The car's tires squealed as his mother suddenly slammed on the brakes. William was flung forward and smacked into the back of his father's seat. The car skidded along the road before stopping.

William cautiously sat up. He looked at his parents, who were motionless, staring out of the windshield. Ahead of them, two lights hovered in the air as if they were waiting for the family. And this time William could see more than just the lights.

A UFO-like object with four propellers hovered in front of them. It was black, had no windows, and was twice as big as the car they were sitting in.

"It looks like some kind of drone," he whispered.

It started to move toward them.

"What do we do now?" his mother asked.

"Back up," his father whispered.

The drone shot toward them at tremendous speed.

"BACK UP!" his father yelled.

His mother put the car in reverse and floored the gas while turning the steering wheel hard so that the car spun around.

"It's over us," William said, leaning over by the window and trying to look up. He could just barely make out the edge of the drone directly above them.

Suddenly there was a bang on the roof, and the whole car jerked upward. The keys hanging from the ignition jingled, then started reaching toward the ceiling as if an invisible force were pulling them. William grabbed his backpack, which was also moving up. The last thing they needed now was for the metal pyramid to start shooting out sparks.

"What's going on?" his father yelled. He was floating over his seat. Only his seat belt prevented him from hitting the car's roof.

William's mother screamed.

William pressed his face against the side window and looked down. They were already high above the ground. The trees beneath them became small matchsticks, and the roads turned into little lines crisscrossing the landscape.

"It must be a magnet," he said. "It picked us up with a magnet."

The drone increased its pace, and soon all William could see of the world below was a blur of green and brown and blue.

His mother was still clutching the steering wheel. But they were trapped. And up here there was nothing they could do to get away.

6

A couple of hours later they were still in the air. The propellers hummed furiously, and the strong side winds rattled the drone. William had tried to figure out what direction they were going, but all he could see below was a vast ocean.

His mother was initially hysterical, convinced that the magnet would let go of them, and it was all his father could do to calm her down.

William leaned back in his seat. He focused on his breathing. Most of the panic he had felt was gone now.

The sun was finally coming up on the horizon.

His mother was quiet. She lay with her head on the steering wheel, not saying a word. Maybe she was asleep. Or maybe she'd just given up. His father was still hovering halfway up to the ceiling, held down only by his seat belt.

"There!" his father exclaimed, pointing. "Land."

William straightened up again. Sure enough, over there, a strip of coastline came into view way ahead of them. They sat in silence, watching as the coastline grew and became clearer the closer they got.

And soon William recognized it: the white cliffs of Dover.

"We're in England," he announced.

His father nodded.

After flying over land for an hour, the tone of the propellers changed, becoming deeper. It sounded like they'd slowed down and were flying lower. William pressed his face to the window and looked out.

A large white building towered high above the fields below them. An enormous park extended out behind the building. William could see the wind rustling the tree leaves and creating small waves on the shiny pond in the middle of the park. The whole area was surrounded by a tall fence, and a long gravel road led from the wrought-iron gates up to the main entrance of the white building.

"It's the Institute," William said.

His parents exchanged looks.

"They could at least have told us they were behind this," his father grumbled. "Then we wouldn't have had to spend the whole night with our hearts in our throats."

William agreed. It *was* strange that Fritz Goffman had basically had them kidnapped. He decided to ask Goffman about this when they arrived. But right now, the relief at learning that the Institute had fetched them far outweighed his anger at how it had been done.

A short time later the car was carefully deposited on the gravel outside the Institute's front entrance. With a clank, the magnet released, and his father flopped back down.

William opened his door and got out. He looked at the drone, which was already high above them.

It really was a strange way to bring us to the Institute, William thought as the drone disappeared over the roof of the building.

He scanned his surroundings. In spite of everything, it was good to be back. This was what he and his grandfather had been counting down to every morning.

His mother got out of the car and looked around. "I've only seen this in pictures in Grandpa's old photo album. I . . ." Her words trailed off as the Institute's huge front doors swung open.

"Did you have a nice trip?" a deep voice inquired.

William recognized it right away. He turned and spotted the tall figure of Fritz Goffman, leaning on his white cane at the top of the broad stone staircase. He was accompanied by his two chauffeurs.

"No . . . we didn't have a nice trip," William's mother

said, crossing her arms defiantly. "It was actually very uncomfortable."

"Oh?" Goffman said. He continued down the stairs, stopped next to William, and gave him a friendly pat on the shoulder.

"I'm Fritz Goffman," he said, introducing himself to William's mother, "head of the Institute."

"I know who you are," William's mom said. "I've seen you in pictures."

William looked at Goffman. There was something about him . . . something strange, out of place. William couldn't put his finger on it, but something was different, something in his eyes.

"We were hunted like animals," William's father said, sticking his head out the passenger-side window. "By that flying food processor."

William's mother continued complaining, but Goffman appeared to be thinking about other things. Instead of responding, he pulled a slip of paper out of his pocket, read it, then folded it meticulously before returning it to his pocket. When William's mom was done talking, it was quiet for a moment.

"I'm truly sorry," Goffman eventually said. "My instructions were for you to be treated with care. When we heard what had happened to your house, I thought it would be best to get you here as quickly as possible, and the drone happened to be in the area."

"Those drones clearly weren't made for human transport!" William's father barked from the car.

"I know," Goffman said with a flat face. "We haven't had them for very long. But they're over a large portion of the world now. The Institute uses them for various tasks, mostly transporting archeological findings. They're not used to transporting people."

"How did you know that something had happened to our house?" William's father asked.

"We keep an eye on you. Or, on William, to be precise. And after everything that happened with the Crypto Portal, we've been extra vigilant. When someone broke into your house, we received immediate notification here at the Institute. Unfortunately, we didn't get there in time to see who it was."

"Who do you suspect?" William's father asked.

"Far too early to say," Goffman responded offhandedly.

He waved to his chauffeurs, who were waiting at the top of the stairs. "Could you help Mr. Wenton out?" He gestured to William's father, who was still sitting in the car. "And be careful. They've been through enough."

The chauffeurs walked over to the car, lifted William's father out, and supported him between them. He hung there like a big baby, not looking particularly pleased.

"Did the break-in have anything to do with the Institute?" William's father asked.

"No," Goffman said, staring at him. "Of course not."

"But you *were* spying on us?" William's father said, sounding irritated.

"For your own safety," Goffman said, glancing at William. "When you live with the world's best code breaker, I'm afraid that's a necessary evil. We can't let anything happen to him." Goffman took a deep breath. "We can discuss this more after you've had a chance to rest. I'm sure you must be hungry? And we'll arrange a new exoskeleton for you," Goffman said, pointing to William's dad. "We've developed a new model that I think you're going to like."

"Forget about that," William's father said. But William could tell that he was torn.

"The new exoskeleton is kinetic," Goffman continued. "It'll charge as you move."

"I know what kinetic means," William's father grumbled.

"The chauffeurs will take you up to our new spa wing, where you can relax," Goffman said, nodding to the chauffeurs, who turned and carried William's father up the stairs.

William's mother hung back for a moment, then looked over at William. "I think I ought to go with him," she said, glancing at the two figures carrying William's father into the building. "And I'm sure the two of you have a lot to discuss."

William nodded.

"They'll be in a better mood after they've had a chance

to rest a bit," Goffman said, walking over to the car and picking William's backpack up off the backseat. "Is this all you brought?"

"Yes," William replied. "Everything else was destroyed."

"Well," Goffman said. "That's what happens when someone uses a pulping detector."

"A pulping detector?" William repeated.

"Whoever went to your house, they were looking for something," Goffman continued. "And they obviously used a pulping detector. It's a very efficient way to search, but extremely destructive. You program in what you want it to find. Then the pulping detector mills through everything it comes across and doesn't stop until it finds what it's looking for."

"We need to find out who broke in," William said.

"We're working on that," Goffman replied, glancing down at the backpack. "You didn't by any chance happen to receive a package recently, did you? Anyone come to see you or get in touch? Anything a little out of the ordinary maybe?"

William hesitated. "Well, actually . . . ," he mumbled. He looked at the backpack that Goffman was clutching in his hands. "Can I have my backpack, please?"

William tried to take it, but Goffman wouldn't let go. Then he appeared to take a breath and released it. William unzipped the main pocket and carefully pulled out the pyramid-shaped package.

"I received this."

"Oh," Goffman said. "May I see?"

William heard Goffman's voice quivering.

"Be careful," William said, and handed it to him. "It makes sparks."

Goffman reached out with both hands and cautiously took the package.

"Where did you get this?"

"It came by mail," William said. There was something about the way Goffman was acting that made William wary. He already regretted showing him the package.

"I think I'll deliver this to the laboratory for examination," Goffman whispered, as if he didn't want to disturb the pyramid.

"How did you know that I'd received something?" William asked.

"I just put two and two together," Goffman said without lifting his eyes off the package in his hands. "Whoever broke into your house was probably looking for this. But obviously, they didn't find it."

He turned without another word and walked up the stone stairs and into the Institute.

7

William followed Goffman into the spacious entrance hall.
People and robots of all sizes and shapes were scurrying
back and forth. William spotted several kids who looked like
new candidates. They were walking in groups of seven and
wearing Institute uniforms: purple blazers and blue pants.

"Now that Abraham Talley is no longer down in the
basement, we've lowered our security level," Goffman said,
sounding pleased. "And we've brought in new candidates.
Everything's almost back to normal."

A group of candidates walked by. Some of them snuck
a peek at William and then put their heads together, whispering. William was happy to see that they were each carrying an orb. All candidates were assigned a personal orb
when they arrived at the Institute. The orbs functioned like

puzzle-keys with ten levels that the candidates had to solve. As the levels were solved, the orb took on new properties while granting its owner access to additional areas within the Institute. When the security level had been raised to five because Cornelia had shown up, the orbs had all been repossessed, but now it looked like the Institute had released the orbs again.

"But what happened to the stairs?" William asked, giving Goffman a questioning look.

The wide stone staircase leading to the second floor had been replaced by two escalators.

"Oh, that was my idea," Goffman said. "Much more efficient than what was here before."

"Uh . . . okay . . ." William wasn't sure if he liked the new escalators.

"What about the step bot?" William thought of the cute little robot that steadfastly used to walk up and down the stairs, with rather variable success.

"It turned out to be completely impracticable," Goffman said tersely. "So it was retired."

"Retired?" William asked. "What does that mean?"

"That it will have a well-deserved rest." Goffman smiled. "Besides, there's no need for step bots with escalators."

William stood there, taking in all the activity around him. Two glossy, highly polished robots wheeled by. They were totally white and shone in the light from the ceiling.

"Are those new too?" he asked.

But Goffman was already heading toward the escalators and didn't reply.

"Excuse me," said a voice from beside William.

He peered down and saw a shiny, flat, white robot that had stopped by his feet. It looked like a mechanical flatfish, maybe a flounder.

"Could you move?" it said. "I haven't vacuumed where you're standing."

"Vacuumed?" William said, confused. This was yet another robot he hadn't seen before. "Uh, what are you?"

"One of the next generation vacuum bots," the robot said proudly.

"What happened to the old ones?" William asked.

"Retired," the vacuum bot replied. "The next generation is much better. Can you move?"

"Are you coming?" Goffman called from over by the escalators.

William started to more forward when a voice stopped him.

"Are you William Wenton?"

William turned toward a group of boys and girls his own age. They were looking at him with curiosity. Some of the girls giggled.

"Well, are you?" one of the girls asked, and smiled expectantly. "Are you William Wenton?"

"Uh . . . ," William hesitantly responded.

"We know all about you," another girl said. "And what you did . . . how you found Abraham Talley in London . . . and what happened in the Himalayas . . . and . . ."

"Can you solve my orb?" one of the boys interrupted.

"Not now, folks," Goffman yelled. "You can speak with William more another time."

William walked over to Goffman.

"How do they know who I am?" he said, looking back.

"You're a bit of a hero around here now," Goffman said, and stepped onto the up escalator.

"Why?" William asked, following him.

"I'll show you." Goffman smiled slyly.

When they reached the top, Goffman proceeded down the hallway. He approached a large glass display case almost ceremoniously.

William stopped. He stood there staring at the large neon letters in front of him.

THE CRYPTO PORTAL: A SUMMARY

Beneath that was something he recognized right away: an old, dented orb.

It was the orb Cornelia Strangler had tricked William into using to activate the Crypto Portal. Next to it he spotted a picture of himself—beside an enormous picture of Goffman. It said THE HEROES OF THE HIMALAYAS. William was taken aback. He glanced over at Goffman, who was staring at something that made William gasp. It wasn't possible. It couldn't be true. A chill ran down his spine, and he started shivering. In front of him sat Cornelia's lethal, mechanical hand.

"Wh-wh-wh-why . . . ," stammered William. He couldn't believe what he was seeing. "Why is *that* here . . . on display?"

"To remind us of what happened in the Himalayas," Goffman said. "It's important that we not forget, and that we learn from our mistakes."

"But . . . ," William continued. "That hand is dangerous . . . lethal! Shouldn't it be locked in a vault or something?" He could almost hear the loud beeping sound it had emitted every time Cornelia had powered it up.

"But the portal was destroyed," Goffman said. "And Cornelia is gone. These things no longer constitute any danger. Besides, this is reinforced, bulletproof, atomic-blast-proof glass."

Goffman pointed into the case. "And there you are."

William glanced at his picture again. It was much smaller than the one of Goffman. And it was black and white.

"We're in the history books," Goffman said.

Goffman's voice sounded dreamy. William looked at him curiously. Goffman was still staring at that mechanical hand, which blinked dimly inside the case.

Suddenly he heard a familiar voice say, "William?"

He turned around and spotted Iscia walking toward him with a group of candidates.

She flung her arms around his neck and hugged him so tight that William felt dizzy.

"It's so good to see you!" she exclaimed. Then she pointed to the cluster of seven candidates standing behind her. They were his age, maybe a little younger. "These are new candidates. They arrived today. I've just given them a little tour."

William nodded to them and smiled.

"That's you," one of the boys said, pointing to the picture inside the display case. He was about to say something more but was interrupted by Iscia.

"You guys are free for the rest of the day," she said.

The little group turned around and walked over to the escalators.

"I should get to the lab and examine this," Goffman said, holding out the package. "And I'm sure you two have a lot of catching up to do." He gave the display one final glance, then walked away.

Inside the case, the rows of buttons on Cornelia's hand pulsed weakly. It almost looked as if it were breathing.

8

"What do you think about this?" Iscia asked, waving at the case.

"I don't really understand why Goffman would put Cornelia's hand on display or why he would hang up a picture of himself . . . ," William said.

"No one does," Iscia whispered.

"Huh," William said.

She was about to say something but stopped when two white, humanlike robots rolled past. William recognized them from the lobby. Iscia waited until the robots were a distance down the hallway before she continued.

"Gossip bots," she said. "They keep an eye on the display. Actually, they watch everything that happens and listen to everything that gets said at the Institute. And then they report all of it directly to Goffman. We can't talk privately here; let's go to your room. I have a lot to tell you."

William glanced over at Iscia as they walked. It seemed like an eternity since they'd sat together on the plane ride back from the Himalayas. He hadn't seen her since they had parted ways at the airport.

Her black hair had grown longer. And she was still a little taller than him.

"I didn't think you were coming back for a couple more weeks," she said.

"That's right," William said. "But someone broke into our house."

"Broke in?" Iscia was shocked. "Who?"

"Dunno. But . . ." William looked around to make sure no one could hear them. "The flash drive with my grandfather on it is gone."

"Huh?" Iscia abruptly stopped walking. "The flash drive he gave you in the Himalayas?"

William nodded, and now it was his turn to pull her along.

"But luckily Benjamin has a backup. I have to get hold of it. I think Grandpa knows something about all the strange things that have happened."

Iscia was surprised. "Benjamin . . . ," she mumbled.

William knocked on the door to his room. He was looking forward to talking to the door again.

"Who's there?" a voice replied in a monotone.

"It's me," William answered.

"Me . . . who?" said the door.

"Me," William repeated, surprised. His door sounded different—flatter, more metallic. "It's me . . . William."

"Do you have clearance?" the door asked. It sounded completely uninterested.

William looked questioningly at Iscia.

"They upgraded the software for all the doors," Ischia whispered. "Didn't Goffman tell you that?"

"I'm next generation," the door said. "The old one was outdated and has been retired."

"Not it, too," William said, disappointed. "What's going on here anyway?"

"A lot," Iscia replied.

A hatch in the door opened and a robot hand with a forehead scanner appeared.

"Lean forward," the door instructed.

William leaned forward. The scanner glowed green.

"Cleared." The door swung open with a click.

They proceeded into the room.

William stopped and looked around. Luckily, the room looked the way it should. His bed was over by the window. The desk and chair were there. The bookshelf was there too, but with some new books on it. William leaned forward and read the titles: *Alternative History, The Technology of the Pyramids*, and *The Earth: A Spaceship*. He'd have to take a closer look at those.

He walked over to the window and peered out. The bars that had been there the last time had been removed. Aside from two shiny, white lawn mower bots, the park looked normal.

"Why have all the robots been replaced?" William asked, turning back to Iscia, who had sat down on the bed.

Iscia put her finger over her lips and gestured for William to come sit down beside her.

She leaned over to him.

"They can hear us," she whispered, and pointed to the door.

William nodded. He grabbed the comforter and pulled it over them. Iscia smiled. "Goffman decided that all the robots need to be upgraded," Iscia whispered. "He said the Institute needs to continue to evolve. There are a lot of people who disagree with him. The new ones are way too efficient and devoid of charm." William nodded silently. From what he had seen since he'd been back, he knew what she meant.

"Did Goffman say anything about Benjamin?" she whispered.

"Like what?" William whispered back.

"That he left. Quit."

"Quit?" William exclaimed in a hushed tone. "Why?"

"I don't really know. He argued with Goffman after the alarm went off."

"What alarm?" William was surprised.

"Haven't you heard?" Iscia whispered. "The Orbulator Agent is out?"

William had no idea what she was talking about. "The Obu-what-er? Huh?"

Iscia took a deep breath. "The Orbulator Agent. He's out. And the day after that, Benjamin quit . . . or . . . well, he disappeared."

"Disappeared?" William repeated.

"Yes. One day he was just gone. According to Goffman, he quit and left. A little weird that he didn't tell any of the rest of us."

A horrible thought popped into William's head.

"What about the backup?" he said. "If Benjamin quit . . . who has the backup?"

"Dunno," Iscia said. "But we need to find that out. Possibly Goffman?"

They sat there in silence for a bit. William felt a shiver run down his spine.

"What's an orbulator agent?" he said after a moment.

Iscia was about to explain when the door interrupted her.

"What are you two whispering about?"

"Nothing." Iscia pulled the comforter off and stood up.

"Gotta go. I have to give a tour to another new group of candidates soon. Busloads of them are arriving every single day." She opened the door and walked out.

Lost in thought, William watched her go.

Had Benjamin really disappeared? What alarm were they talking about? And what in the world was an orbulator agent? The questions were piling up.

William stood.

"I wonder when dinner is," he mumbled.

"You ask too many questions," the door replied dryly.

9

Gray moonlight beamed through the small window and into the dark room. Outside, the distant hum from guard bots was the only sound in the quiet night. William lay on his bed still wearing the clothes he'd arrived in. He had been lying like this for hours.

He had hoped Iscia would come back. He still had a lot of questions and no answers. He needed someone to talk to. But Iscia didn't seem to know very much either. William shifted his position so he could look out the window. Surely his grandfather would have been able to help.

William really wanted to talk to Goffman, too, but the man's behavior had been so strange. It was almost as if he was a different person—scrapping all the old robots, dispatching gossip bots to spy on people—and then there was the way he had transported them to the Institute with the drone. . . . It was all totally out of character. It was bizarre—scary even! And to top it all off, Benjamin had disappeared.

For a brief moment, William thought about finding his parents. He hadn't seen them since they'd arrived at the Institute. They were probably having a good time down at the spa, but they would start worrying again. He decided to leave them alone until he had a better idea about what was happening at the Institute.

"There is someone at the door," the door said flatly.

William sat up in bed. "Who?"

"I don't know," the door replied. "No one is allowed into or out of the rooms after eleven o'clock."

William got up.

"I have to report this to Mr. Goffman," the door added. "This is a security matter, and—" There was a zap from outside the door, and sparks shot out of the speaker. The lights in the room blinked a couple of times.

"Door?" William said, but there was no response. "Door? Are you there?"

William got up, his eyes fixed on the door.

With a click, it opened, and the silhouette of a figure came into view. It was a man.

William backed away.

"Quickly, we have to talk," the man said. He closed the door behind him, came into the room, and stopped.

William bumped into the wall next to the bed. The man had blond hair and a round face. His pale skin was wrinkled and old. William was sure he'd never seen him before in his life. All the same . . . he thought there was something familiar about him. Something about the way he moved.

"We don't have much time before they notice that the door is out of commission," the old man said, scratching his chin nervously.

And suddenly William knew exactly who it was. But how could that be?

"Benjamin?" he whispered.

"Darn it!" the man said. He raised one hand and pushed something at the back of his skull. The whole head flashed a couple of times before it started to morph. The hair changed from pale blond to black, and the face became longer and younger.

A couple of seconds later, Benjamin stood before William. He was wearing some kind of metallic headband.

"Ugh, this hologram mask . . . it would be much better if it changed the whole body. If only I had time."

"Iscia said you'd left the Institute."

"In a way, I have," Benjamin said, nodding.

"What do you mean?"

"I quit," Benjamin said. "Or rather, Goffman fired me. But I didn't leave. How could I, under these circumstances?

I'm in hiding, and you can't tell anyone you talked to me. Clear?"

William nodded. "My house was broken into," he said. "The flash drive with my grandfather on it is gone."

"You don't need to worry about that," Benjamin said. "I have a backup in my office. We'll fix that later. We have much more important stuff to talk about. . . ." He paused, staring expectantly at William.

"Well, where is it?" Benjamin asked, looking around. "The package? I came here as soon as I heard about it."

"The package?" William said.

"The pyramid . . . it's about this big." Benjamin demonstrated with his hands. "And covered with a strange symbols. Supposedly."

"Goffman took it," William said.

Benjamin just stood there. He looked disappointed. And angry. William realized that letting Goffman take the package had probably been a mistake.

"You gave it to *him*?" Benjamin clenched his fists.

"Yes," William said. "Or rather, he took it from me."

"Then you have to get it back." Benjamin's voice was insistent.

"What is that pyramid?" William asked. He needed answers.

"It's a code." Benjamin lowered his voice. "One of the most extraordinary and important codes in the world. It's been hidden for eons. Guarded by the Orbulator Agent. But now the Orbulator Agent has surfaced and is among us. There could only be one reason for that."

"What?" William asked.

"I expect that you're the one he wants to give it to. Only, now Goffman has it."

"Would you please explain, Benjamin."

"I'll tell you everything. But first: Who gave you the pyramid?"

"A mailman," William replied.

"What did he look like? This mailman." Benjamin's whole face was alight with curiosity.

"He was a little taller than you. And thinner. He drove an old mail truck and was very pale. Almost completely white in the face."

"That *must* have been him," Benjamin said with an enthusiastic grin.

"Who?"

"The Orbulator Agent." Benjamin lowered his voice even more now and glanced quickly around the room. "This is huge!"

"And who *is* the Orbulator Agent?" William asked impatiently.

Benjamin took a deep breath, then fixed his eyes on William again.

"Many years ago we discovered a peculiar parchment

in the Depository for Impossible Archeology here at the Institute. It was hidden inside a very old Egyptian statue. We carbon-dated it to more than two thousand years old. The parchment described an android that called itself the Orbulator Agent."

Benjamin paused and looked at William, as if he wanted to make sure he was really paying attention.

"The parchment said that this android guarded a code that would access an ancient weapon." Benjamin glanced nervously at the door.

"What kind of weapon?" William asked, his heart pounding.

"The only weapon that could defeat luridium if it should ever return to earth." Benjamin took another deep breath before hurrying on. "The old parchment described how the Orbulator Agent's sole purpose was to guard this code, waiting for a person who can solve it and access the weapon."

"And the pyramid?" William asked.

"I believe that the pyramid is the code," Benjamin said.

William stood quietly, giving himself some time to digest this new information.

"The same pyramid that I had?"

"I think so!" Benjamin stopped and looked at the door as if he had heard something. "The package you received is the code. If you solve that, you'll access the weapon. And thereby the only thing in the whole world that can stop Abraham Talley."

"B–but why did I get it?" William stuttered. "Why now?"

"I can think of only one reason for the agent to have given the pyramid to you, William," Benjamin said, and paused. "Mankind is in great jeopardy."

Suddenly William understood what Benjamin was trying to tell him.

"You think that Abraham will return to earth!"

Benjamin nodded silently.

A shiver ran through William's body. Just saying the name Abraham Talley gave him chills. Was there really something that could stop Abraham and the luridium? Did the Orbulator Agent want him to use this ancient weapon that Benjamin was talking about? Whatever it was?

Benjamin inhaled. "We have to get the pyramid back. There are people out there who don't want you to solve the code. . . ."

Benjamin was about to say something more, but a sudden noise made him turn back to the door. Now William could hear the sound of electric motors approaching. He knew right away what that meant: A bunch of guard bots was coming.

In one quick motion, Benjamin stuck his hand under his jacket and pulled out a metallic headband like the one he was wearing. He tossed it to William.

"Take this," he said, backing toward the door. "You're going to need it."

Benjamin activated his own hologram mask, and once again his head transformed into an old man's.

"You have to get that pyramid back. We'll help you."

"Who is we?" William asked.

But it was too late. Benjamin was gone.

10

There was a knock on the door. It was still out of commission, so William had to open it manually. A group of brand-new guard bots stood outside. They were armed with passivators. William shuddered at the sight of them. He had been paralyzed by those things before. He hated them.

"Step aside. We're here to investigate a safety breach," one of the guard bots said, and wheeled into the room so quickly that William had to jump out of the way.

In its hand, the guard bot held something that looked almost like a high-tech clothes iron, and now it raised the tool to scan the room.

William glanced over at the bed. The hologram mask Benjamin had left for him was sitting there. If the guard bot had time to scan the whole room, it would be found.

"Uh . . . everything's fine here," William said. "But I heard someone running down the hall."

The guard bot turned to him.

"Someone was running?"

"Yes, it sounded as if they were running away. They were probably scared because they heard you coming."

The guard bot looked satisfied and turned to the other bots waiting outside the small room.

"Come on—we have to find the intruder," it said. The guard bot dashed off down the hallway.

William turned a corner and kept going down a long hall. Had Benjamin gone this way? If he was still here at the Institute, where was he hiding?

It was the middle of the night, but William still hadn't slept. He'd just been thinking over everything Benjamin had said—and everything he hadn't had a chance to say! William had to find him.

He turned left at the end of the hallway and suddenly found himself at the Crypto Portal display. A faint glow was coming from the glass display case, but the neon sign had been turned off. He still couldn't understand why Goffman had created an exhibit about what had happened in the Himalayas. The only thing the Crypto Portal reminded William of was everything that had gone wrong, how Abraham Talley had traveled through the portal, and how Cornelia had killed his grandfather.

William felt sick when he thought about it. Luckily, Cornelia obliterated herself with her own hand, the very same hand that was now on display inside the glass case.

William walked closer.

He could see the old orb. And the picture of himself, just below the larger picture of Goffman.

But something was missing.

Cornelia's mechanical hand was gone.

That couldn't be possible. The atomic-bomb-proof glass display cabinet was perfectly intact. There was no sign of a break-in or vandalism. And yet the hand was gone.

William shuddered. This was what he'd been afraid of.

He knew that the hand could move about on its own. He had seen it himself, on the plane to the Himalayas. He checked the thick glass door again. It was locked. The hand would have needed a key to get out. No, someone had to have removed it, but who?

He had to find out, and the only way to do that would be to hide and hope that whoever had taken it would put it back in its place before morning.

He hurried over to a dark corner and stopped in front of a large statue of a woman with wings holding an orb in one hand. William squeezed in behind the statue and sat down. From there he had a direct view of the glass display case.

He'd have to continue his search for Benjamin tomorrow. Right now he needed to stay awake and see if someone brought the hand back.

William awoke with a start and sat up. Golden morning sunlight poured through the big window above him. He peeked out from behind the statue. The place was crawling with people and robots. Two girls stood by the display case, pointing at it and discussing something.

William stood up and jogged over to the case on stiff legs.

"You're William Wenton," one of the girls said.

William didn't respond. He was staring at what was lying next to the old orb inside the case.

Cornelia Strangler's mechanical hand was back.

11

In the enormous dining hall, server bots were wheeling between tables. Brand-new candidates sat in small groups eating fried eggs, sausages, toast, and pancakes. Everyone was talking and laughing, blissfully ignorant that Cornelia's hand had disappeared and then turned up again overnight.

"William Wenton," a voice said flatly.

A white server bot holding a tray of freshly baked rolls stopped beside him.

"Yes?" William replied.

"Come with me," the robot said, and then continued rolling along. "You sit at table seven. They're waiting for you."

In well-practiced slalom-like motions, the server bot rolled between all the people hurrying back and forth to the buffet. It raised its tray high over its head and balanced it without a single roll tumbling off.

William followed it to table seven. There he saw Iscia and the other candidates he had met the day before. They were already halfway through their breakfast.

William sat at the table, and a plate of pancakes and jam was placed in front of him. Next to his plate there was a large glass of Mars juice.

"Is it true that you have attacks that let you solve impossible codes?" a blond girl asked as she took a bite out of a large bun so freshly baked it was still steaming. She made a face.

William nodded, his cheeks burning. All the candidates around the table stared at him with curiosity. He looked down at his plate and tried to concentrate on the pancakes.

"Well, they're not really attacks then, are they?" one of the boys said. "I mean, if they help you crack codes, then they're more like some kind of assistance?"

"In a way," William said, and took a big bite of pancake. He spat it right back out again. It tasted like old cardboard.

"The food isn't that good lately," Iscia said, pushing her own plate away.

"What happened?" William had a disgusting taste in his mouth.

"New cook bots," Iscia said. "They're still in training."

William wasn't ready to give up on his pancakes yet. Maybe the second bite would taste better. He took a new bite, but only managed to chew it three times before he had to spit it back out. It tasted like a mixture of wet toilet paper and Play-Doh.

"Why do you think Abraham Talley was the one who found the luridium when they were digging those tunnels under London?" another girl said.

"I think it was a total accident," Iscia responded quickly.

"Me too," William said, glancing over at her.

"And then he went completely crazy and tried to kill you before he traveled to outer space through the Crypto Portal?" another boy said.

"Mm-hmm . . ." William pushed his plate away, admitting pancake defeat.

"Are you done with that?" a tidy bot asked, snatching the plate away before William had a chance to answer.

"Aren't you afraid that the same thing will happen to you?" the girl with blond hair asked.

"That what will happen?" William said to her.

"That you'll go crazy?" the girl said. "Or turn evil?"

William didn't know what to say.

"William doesn't have as much luridium in him as Abraham Talley," Ischia said.

"We know that," the girl said. "William's only half-luridium."

"But what do you think happened to Freddy?" a boy

WILLIAM WENTON and the LOST CITY

with really shiny braces said. "Why did he enter the Crypto Portal with Abraham?"

"I don't know," William said.

"That's a big mystery," Iscia continued.

"I'm totally convinced that Abraham Talley made it wherever he wanted to go," a girl with short hair and glasses said. "And soon he'll be on his way back here with the luridium to destroy us."

Everyone stopped talking while two gossip bots rolled by.

"Enough about that." Ischia looked around to see if anyone had noticed what they were talking about. "We shouldn't talk about that. Not here."

They sat in silence for a bit.

William looked at the others around the table. They were staring at him like he was some kind of hero. Something that William didn't feel like at all, and he didn't like being treated like a celebrity. It seemed like every one of the new candidates knew him. How could he sneak around at the Institute when he has a celebrity? He had to figure out a way.

He stole a glance at Iscia. He was eager for breakfast to end so that he could take her aside and tell her what he had discovered during the night. He also wanted to fill her in on what Benjamin had told him.

"William," a voice said. William looked up and spotted Goffman. "Can I have a word with you?"

William stood.

"See you later," Iscia said with a smile.

William nodded and followed Goffman into the hallway outside the dining hall.

"Where are we going?" William asked.

Goffman merely said, "Your parents are waiting outside," and kept moving.

"Are they leaving?" William asked anxiously.

"Yes," Goffman said without looking at him.

Goffman led the way through the main lobby, and William had a chance to study him from behind. Was he limping a little? It looked like it. And his hair definitely wasn't as neat as it usually was. But, what with Benjamin gone, Goffman probably had extra work to do. That must be taking a toll on him. Now that he was alone with Goffman, William had gotten what he had wished for: a chance to find out how much Goffman knew about the stuff Benjamin had told him.

"I . . . ," William began.

"What?" Goffman asked.

"Well, I was just wondering . . . Did you find out anything more about that pyramid?"

"Not much," Goffman said, and kept walking. "We need some more time to study it."

"What do you think it is?" William continued.

"I don't know. It could be anything."

Goffman's answers sounded rehearsed and flat. Like he had prepared for William's questions.

"And what about the Orbulator Agent?" William knew that the name would catch Goffman off guard and get some kind of real, unrehearsed reaction from him.

Goffman stopped, turned around slowly, and looked sternly at William. His eyes were dark and angry, but then his face broke out in a huge grin.

"So, you've heard of him? Strange. I thought—" Goffman stopped himself, then smiled even more broadly and ruffled William's hair. "The Orbulator Agent is just an old myth. No one believes he actually exists. You shouldn't listen to all the gossip here at the Institute. People have no idea what they're talking about."

"But isn't there an old parchment that says that—" William began, but Goffman cut him short.

"There's no Orbulator Agent—do you hear me?" He turned and proceeded out of the building.

William understood that he wouldn't get any more answers from Goffman and decided to back off. He had to figure out where the pyramid was being kept, and then he had to steal it back. The Orbulator Agent had given it to him for a reason.

Outside, William's parents were waiting by the car. William stopped when he caught sight of his father. He wasn't wearing his exoskeleton anymore. He was standing there in a new suit, grinning from ear to ear. This was the first time in years that William had seen his father standing up without any form of visible assistive device.

"What do you think?" His dad held out his arms to show off his new suit. But William knew that what he was really showing off was that he could stand up entirely on his own.

"This is a tremendous advance," Goffman said, pointing to William's father.

His father unbuttoned his shirt to reveal what was underneath the suit. It gleamed gray.

"He's wearing a completely new type of ultrasuit," Goffman explained. "It functions as an exoskeleton. Electrical impulses multiply the existing muscular strength of the person wearing it."

His father buttoned the shirt again and grinned at William.

"It's really cool, don't you think?" he said.

William nodded. He'd never seen his father look so pleased.

"Time to go," William's mother said, opening the car door. She glanced at William.

"This is what we've always dreamed of," his father said. "Being able to return to England to visit friends and family. We have a lot of catching up to do."

"We're going to visit your father's brother in Wales. We

haven't seen him since we moved to Norway." Mother smiled at William. "Your father just talked to him on the phone. He can't wait to see you."

There was a short silence. And William just stood there for a little while looking at his parents. He was unsure of what to do next. Did they want him to go with them? He glanced up at Goffman but got nothing from his expressionless face.

"I'm—going with you?" he stammered, turning to look at his parents.

"Well, of course," his father blurted out. Like anything else was a complete impossibility. "Goffman didn't tell you?"

William shook his head.

"We all think this is for the best," Goffman said. "It's not safe for you here right now. Taking a little trip with your parents is the best you can do. Let that big brain of yours have a well-deserved rest." Goffman ruffled William's hair with his bony fingers again.

"Well, we'd better get going," his mother said. "I don't like driving in the dark." She motioned for William to get in the car. Then she got in behind the wheel.

Reluctantly William made his way over to the car, opened the door, and climbed into the backseat. He looked out at Goffman, who just stood there. William thought he saw a glint of a smirk on his lips.

William's father sat down in front.

His mother started the car, and they began to drive.

"It's probably best this way," she said. "So many strange things are happening at the Institute. We'll go spend some time with the family. You can relax. Save up your strength."

The engine roared as she placed her foot on the accelerator, and William was pushed into his seat. He could hear how the gravel shot out from under the rear tires. He looked back at Goffman, who still stood there. Like he wanted to make sure that William really did leave. Confused, William scratched his forehead. Why was Goffman sending him away? And why had he taken the strange pyramid from him when the postman had specifically said that it was for William's eyes only? Something wasn't right.

The car stopped in front of the big wrought-iron gates that marked the boundary of the Institute's property. The two gates slowly slid open, and the car kept going.

William put his hands in his lap, thinking like crazy. He needed to get the pyramid back. There must be a good reason why the strange man had given it to him. William *needed* to return to the Institute.

William thrust his hand into his pants pocket and pulled out the folded metallic headband that Benjamin had given him.

"Stop the car!" he said.

12

William ran down the road.

It had been surprisingly easy to convince his parents to let him out. True, he had flagrantly lied and told them he would follow them shortly in one of the Institute's private planes, but they'd believed him because he'd said that he had to go get Grandpa's backup, and it would take a little time to get it restarted. That part actually wasn't a lie, but the rest of it wasn't so easy.

Sneaking into the Institute would be hard. A camera mounted on top of the gate at the Institute was panning back and forth. William knew it would be impossible to get in without being filmed, and the guard bots had probably already been informed that William Wenton wasn't supposed to be staying there. He had to use the hologram mask Benjamin had given him. And find Iscia. He couldn't do this alone, but he had a plan.

William put the metal headband on his head and pushed the button. A gleam of light shot out in front of his eyes. Otherwise, he didn't notice much of anything. He touched his face but felt only his own skin. Was the hologram mask not working?

He spotted a puddle a little way away, walked to it, and checked his reflection. He jumped when he saw the face staring back up at him from the dark water. It was an old man with wrinkly skin, a big mustache, and white hair. He looked like Albert Einstein. It was ridiculous. William couldn't walk around with an old man's head on a young boy's body. His cover would be blown right away.

He pushed the button on the back of the headband again. And with that, his face changed, becoming a woman's. He tried again. His faced morphed yet again. This time it was a boy with red hair and freckles looking back up at him. *Perfect,* he thought.

Suddenly he heard the rumble of an engine. William turned and spotted a bus coming toward him. He ran to hide behind a bush.

The brakes whined as the bus slowed down, pulled over by the gate, and stopped. William peeked out. A group of kids his own age peered through the windows curiously. More candidates on their way into the Institute.

Before William realized what he was doing, he was running, hunched over, toward the bus. He got there right as it began to move. He jumped up onto the bumper and hung on tight. The bus drove in the gate and bumped along the gravel drive. William was sure he would be discovered—or flung off.

But when the bus stopped in front of the main entrance, he hopped down and hid behind it.

The bus doors opened, and the kids poured out. Soon the area was buzzing with excited voices. William peeked around the corner. He counted fourteen children and one adult.

Emerging from his hiding spot, William snuck over to the group and joined them, tagging along at the very back.

"Is everyone here?" asked the lady standing at the front.

Everyone in the group nodded.

The lady was wearing a purple suit jacket with the Institute's emblem. William had seen her before and was quite sure that she knew who he was. But for the time being, he was safe behind his hologram mask.

"Follow me," the woman said before turning toward the building and climbing the stairs.

It felt very strange to enter the Institute this way, as if this were his first visit. William looked at the others. Their eyes were wide with excitement. If only they knew all the things that were going on here.

"Welcome to the Institute for Post-Human Research," the woman said, flinging her arms wide as they entered the massive lobby.

A gasp ran through the group, then became part of the buzz of human voices and robots that filled the space. Men and women in white coats moved quickly across the room engaged in animated discussions with one another. A group of young candidates displayed their orbs, and a vacuum bot tried to maneuver through the crowd of people and robots to do its job.

"This is where I leave you," the lady continued. "And one of our most trusted field assistants, Iscia, will take over. She'll show you around."

William's heart skipped a beat as Iscia came toward them.

"Welcome!" she said, smiling.

The new candidates followed Iscia through the large hall.

William was still at the very back of the group.

The candidates had looked around wide-eyed as Iscia showed them the main building and the park behind it, and now they were on their way up the escalators. William looked back down at the lobby and spotted a group of guard bots pushing their way through the crowd. Had his presence been discovered?

"This way," Iscia said when they reached the top of the escalator.

The little group followed her over to the Crypto Portal display. She stopped and turned around to face them. William glanced down at the lobby again. The guard bots were stopping random people and identifying them with forehead scanners.

William knew it was only a question of time before the guard bots reached the group he'd entered with, and then it was only a matter of seconds before they discovered him.

"Are you coming?" he heard Iscia call.

She was eyeing William impatiently.

"I can't begin until everyone is ready," she said. "Hurry up."

Iscia turned around to face the Crypto Portal display. She stared at the glass case. It was almost as if she didn't want to tell them what was in there.

"You weren't on the bus," a voice next to William said.

"Huh?" he said, turning around in fear. A young girl was looking at him, her head cocked to the side. His heart started beating faster. Was the game over?

"You didn't come on the bus with the rest of us," the girl said. "Did you lose your group?"

William glanced over at Iscia, but she didn't seem to have heard what the girl had said.

"Yes," he whispered. "I missed the last tour, so I had to come on this one."

"Oh, right," the girl said, nodding like she accepted his explanation.

"Forehead scan," a monotone voice said from behind them.

William turned around. Three guard bots were rolling toward them. The one in the middle was holding a forehead scanner. The other two were armed with passivators.

13

William had to think fast. The guard bot with the forehead scanner stopped in front of the girl who had just spoken to him.

The girl looked around in confusion. She caught William's eye.

William fought his urge to run for it. He had to remain calm. If he was discovered, the game would be up, and he could forget all about getting the pyramid back.

"Lean forward," he said. "They just want to scan your forehead to find out who you are."

The girl gulped and did as William had said. She leaned forward and squeezed her eyes shut.

"It doesn't hurt," William said.

The guard bot placed the scanner to the girl's forehead.

The light blinked red a couple of times before changing to green.

"Cleared," the guard bot said, and turned toward a tall, thin boy. "Forehead scan."

The boy placed his hands behind his back and obediently leaned his upper body forward.

William snuck a peek at Iscia, who was still standing by the display case. He backed his way into the group and waved discreetly, but she didn't see him. She was staring at the tall boy. The forehead scanner lit up in green.

"Cleared," the guard bot pronounced.

William waved more enthusiastically to catch her attention. "Psst," he whispered.

But Iscia still hadn't noticed him. William kept going. Soon he was halfway to her.

"Iscia," he whispered.

Finally she glanced at him.

"You can't leave the group," she whispered. "You risk being passivized."

Of course she didn't recognize him. She just saw an unfamiliar red-haired boy.

But William couldn't give up. He snuck a peek over at the guard bots. They were still busy scanning the rest of the group.

"It's me," William whispered, coming to a stop right next to her.

"Me?" Iscia said. "What are you talking about? Get back there before we both end up passivized."

"It's me!" he whispered again. "William."

"William?" She looked at him as if he were completely crazy.

"William Wenton," he said, leaning toward her.

"Huh?"

"The guards can't find out that it's me," William said. "I'm wearing a hologram mask. You have to help me. I'll explain later."

She still didn't seem to have any idea what he meant.

He was going to have to show her.

William raised one hand and found the button on the back of the metal headband. A quick flash of light shot in front of his face. Iscia's eyes widened. William leaned to the side and looked at his reflection in the glass display case. He had Albert Einstein's head again.

But now it appeared that Iscia understood.

"William?" she whispered, casting a rapid, terrified glace at the guard bots. "Are you the one they're looking for?"

"Goffman thinks that I left with my parents. But I came back." William pushed the button twice more and turned into the red-haired boy again, just in the nick of time.

"You there," the guard bot said.

The guard bot with the forehead scanner approached him. "Forehead scan," it said.

William peeked at Iscia.

"Run," she whispered.

"Huh?" William said.

"Run," she repeated. "I'll stall them." And in a quick motion she hit the alarm button next to the glass display case. Metal walls shot up out of the floor to surround the orb, the picture of William, and Cornelia's hand.

An alarm started howling. The guard bot with the forehead scanner stopped abruptly, peering into the display case. The other two did the same thing.

"We have to meet somehow," William whispered. "I have a lot to tell you." He turned and ran as fast as he could.

14

William sat alone at the far end of the grounds. The cyber-netic garden had been shut down a long time ago. Most of the cages were empty now, but there were still mechanical plants in a few of them. He peered up at the cage beside him. In it was a carnivorous plant, its head drooping. Iron teeth that were as sharp as awls stuck out of its mouth. Luckily, it was deactivated now.

He couldn't believe that this was the only place he felt remotely safe. But right now he needed somewhere to be alone and think. He needed a plan. How was he going to find the pyramid? And how would he find Benjamin? Somehow William just knew that the curious disappearance and return of Cornelia's hand had something to do with all of this.

William jumped when he heard a low clank. Someone was entering the garden. William withdrew, making his way farther toward the back, pressing himself against the cold sprinkler closet there. Was it a guard bot? Had he been discovered? It was too dark for him to be able to see who or what it was, but its eyes glowed a dim red, so it had to be a robot. William glimpsed it again. This wasn't any old robot—it was the argu-bot itself! It stopped on the grassy lawn, then started moving again.

William followed it with his eyes.

Was it safe for him to come out?

He took a few faltering steps.

The argu-bot stopped when it spotted William. It stood there for a while, startled. William remembered that he still had the hologram mask on. He touched the button on the back of his head. There was a zap and a quick flash in front of his face.

The argu-bot's face lit up in recognition.

"It is you," it said, wheeling toward him. When it was a few yards away, it stopped, staring penetratingly at William.

The argu-bot touched its ear. "I found him," it whispered.

Then it gestured to William and said, "You need to come with me. It isn't safe here."

William was taken aback and didn't move.

"Have you been passivized or something?" the argu-bot said. "Hurry up. The others are waiting."

"Who is?" William asked.

"Benjamin and the others," the argu-bot said. "No time for arguing now. I'll be happy to accommodate you on that later." The tall robot turned and started rolling away, back toward the front. "If you stay in here, you'll be passivator food. It's only a matter of time before the guard bots find you. And that would be a situation I couldn't argue you out of."

"How did you find me?" William asked as he ran across the lawn toward the main Institute building.

"There's a transmitter in the hologram mask Benjamin gave you, but I had to be sure," the argu-bot replied. "And I suggest that you remain silent now. We can't be discovered. I need to get you up to the storeroom."

"The storeroom?" William replied.

"Shh!" the argu-bot hissed, still moving toward the Institute building. William felt his body tingling with adrenaline.

They stopped in front of a back door leading into the main building. The argu-bot entered a code into a control panel.

The door emitted a brief beep and slid open. There was an elevator inside. The walls were dirty, and the floor was covered with dry branches and leaves. There was a gash running up one wall. The argu-bot rolled in and waved at William to follow.

According to the panel inside the elevator, the Institute had many more floors than William had realized. He wondered if he would ever get to see them all. The argu-bot had to stretch to press a button high up.

"Going up," a muted female voice announced.

"This elevator is mostly used by the gardener bots," the argu-bot explained.

"Where are we going?" William asked.

"To the Storeroom for Useless Robots," the argu-bot said.

"Useless robots?" William asked.

"That's where Goffman has stowed all the retired robots. It's awful up there. Intolerable conditions."

The elevator stopped, and the doors slid open. The argu-bot rolled out. "Come on," it said. "We don't have much time. We need to take another elevator up to—" The robot didn't have a chance to say anything else before a ray of blue light hit it hard in the chest, causing sparks to fly out in every direction.

The argu-bot wobbled for a few seconds before tipping forward and hitting the floor with a loud clank.

15

The argu-bot lay motionless on the floor, just outside the open door. William quickly surveyed the inside of the elevator car. There was a hatch in the ceiling. He'd seen this in movies plenty of times, but could he do it?

The hum of electrical motors was getting closer. He had to try.

Climbing up, William balanced himself with one foot on each of the railings on either side of the car. He braced himself, then put one hand on the emergency hatch and pushed. It opened.

William stretched, grabbing the edge of the opening with both hands, and pulled himself up. It was hard, but with an enormous amount of effort he was able to get his torso over the edge. Then he pulled his legs up and flipped the hatch shut again just as the hum of the electric motors got even closer.

It was cold and dark on top of the elevator, and William's heart lurched when he noticed that he hadn't managed to close the hatch fully. Through the crack he could see part of the elevator and the argu-bot, which was still lying motionless in the hallway. And if William could see *them* . . . the guard bots would be able to see *him*.

He reached his hand out to close the hatch but instinctively pulled it back again when two guard bots stopped in the hallway just outside the elevator below him. One of them entered the elevator and looked around.

William pulled farther back into the darkness and held his breath.

"There's no one else here," the guard bot announced.

"So it was alone?" the other one said, gesturing at the passivized argu-bot.

"Who?" the first one said.

"That," the other said, poking at the disabled argu-bot with its passivator.

"An older model. Belongs in the storeroom. Probably trying to escape."

"But we heard voices."

The guard bot surveyed the inside of the elevator. "Maybe it was arguing with itself?"

"Robots don't talk to themselves," the other one said. "Everyone knows that."

"I would beg to differ," the argu-bot said.

"It's alive," one of the guard bots said, and pointed its passivator at the argu-bot. "Should I shoot it again?"

"Shoot it if it moves," the other guard bot said as a beam of red light shot out of the head of the guard bot standing right below William. The beam began to scan the elevator, starting at the bottom of the wall and moving systematically up the walls.

William froze. He was only seconds away from being discovered now.

"Happy birthday to you," the argu-bot suddenly began. "Happy birthday, dear . . . bananas . . . cannons . . . cocoa powder . . ."

The red beam disappeared as the guard bot stopped scanning. It turned and studied the old argu-bot.

"Baa baa black sheep . . . yes, sir, yes, sir, three bags . . . baking powder . . . CAKE POWDER!"

"That robot has obviously lost its marbles," the guard bot inside the elevator said. "We'll take it with us. It has to go back to the storeroom anyway before it says something inappropriate."

"Your mother was a tin can!" the argu-bot shouted.

"Okay, that's it," one of the guard bots said, and grabbed hold of one of the argu-bot's arms. "Don't say anything about my mother."

"You don't have a mother," the argu-bot argued. "Because you're a stupid robot."

"You're stupid!" the other guard bot said, and grabbed hold of the other arm. "Now shut up and stay still!"

"And your mother was an iPod," the argu-bot said flatly.

The guard bot pointed its passivator at the argu-bot. There was a quick zap, and the argu-bot fell silent.

William sat in the darkness and watched as the two guard bots dragged the argu-bot away.

"No one talks about our mothers like that," one of the guard bots said. "Even if we don't have any."

William waited until the hum was completely gone before he dared to breathe. His heart was pounding so hard it sounded like a bass drum in his head.

He glanced up at the darkness above him. The elevator shaft continued upward. The small amount of light from the hatch below was just enough to get a vague sense of his surroundings. The cable holding the elevator up was next to him. He grabbed it and stood. He had to make his way upward. The argu-bot had said something about another elevator, but that wasn't an option anymore. If he climbed back down into the elevator, he risked being passivized by guard bots. He put one foot on the wall and, using the cable to pull himself up, started climbing. At school, he had always been good at rope climbing. Something that paid off now.

★ ★ ★

A few minutes later he reached the top of the shaft. He had passed three floors. His body ached, and he was drenched in sweat. He held on to the thick wire with trembling hands and looked down into the dark depths of the elevator shaft below.

There was a double elevator door in front of him. And on the wall next to the door, a mechanical lever marked FOR EMERGENCY ONLY!

Carefully William let go of the cable with one hand and reached for the lever. He grabbed hold of it and, with his remaining strength, pulled it down.

There was a low click from the elevator doors as they slid open to reveal what was on the other side.

A long hallway.

Soon William found himself standing in the same hallway. His legs were shaking, and his palms were burning. He had been so full of adrenaline as he climbed up the cable that he hadn't noticed how much it was taking out of him. Now he just wanted to lie down, but he knew he had to keep going.

He walked rapidly down the hallway. This was obviously a little-used part of the Institute. The floor was covered with a layer of gray dust that swirled up with every step he took. Every once in a while he spotted a footprint in the dust. Some were old, others newer.

He came to the end of the hall and stopped. It was a dead end. He was surrounded by white walls. There was a red *X* painted on the floor.

William stepped over to one wall and ran his hand over the smooth surface. He knocked on a few spots with his knuckles, but the wall sounded solid.

He closed his eyes. If there was a code here, he was very sure the vibrations would turn up.

When nothing happened, he opened his eyes again, walked over to the red *X*, and stood right on the middle of it.

A deep voice boomed out of the ceiling above him, causing him to jump. "Password?"

In the ceiling there was a white hatch the size of a manhole cover. It was almost completely impossible to spot.

"Do you have the password?" the voice asked.

"Uh," William said.

"Uh?" the voice repeated. "That is not the password."

"I'm looking for the Storeroom for Useless Robots," William said. "Is that nearby?"

Silence from the ceiling. William stood there, waiting.

"Hello?" he said.

"William?" the voice asked. "Is that you?"

He recognized that voice.

"Door?" he said.

"William!" the door said.

William lit up. It was his old door.

"What are you doing up here? I thought you'd been retired."

"In a way I have been," the door said. "There's not much action up here."

"I have to get into the storeroom. Benjamin is waiting for me."

"Excellent! That means something is going on."

"What's going on?" William asked.

"Dunno," the door said hesitantly. "A revolution maybe?"

"A revolution?"

"You'll have to ask Benjamin. He's the boss up here."

The hatch in the ceiling opened, and a large glass tube descended and stopped just above William.

"Are you sure you want to go in this way?" the door asked.

"If it leads to the Storeroom for Useless Robots," William replied.

"As you wish."

The tube came down, surrounding William, and stopped when it reached the floor.

"Good luck!" the door said.

And with a *flop*, the tube sucked William up.

16

William landed with a splash in a pool of purple liquid. He sank to the bottom and waved his arms in a desperate attempt to reach the surface. It was frothing and bubbling around him, which made it impossible to tell up from down. The bitter-tasting liquid got in his mouth, and his lungs burned from lack of oxygen. Panic started to take over. He flailed more and more, but to no avail.

Suddenly he felt something grab him and yank him up. He inhaled all the way down into his belly, filling his lungs with fresh air. He rubbed the stuff out of his eyes and blinked a few times before he was able to see where he was.

He was hanging over a pool in a large, white room.

"Decontamination complete," a deep voice announced from a speaker in the ceiling.

William looked over his shoulder and spotted a robotic arm hanging from the ceiling. It had a firm grip on him.

The arm swung him away from the pool and set him on the floor. Then it vanished into a hatch in the ceiling and came back with something that looked like a large hair dryer.

"Initiating drying," the voice from the speaker announced.

The warm air coming out of the hair dryer was blowing so vigorously that William had trouble remaining on his feet.

"Stand still," the dryer instructed, following him. "Let me do my job."

The strength of the air pushed William until he was up against the wall. His clothes flapped so forcefully that he thought they would blow right off.

"Drying complete," the voice announced, and the robotic arm vanished back into the ceiling.

"Ready for storage," the voice said.

William heard a deep rumble behind him. He turned around and saw the wall separate in the middle. The entire wall was an enormous door. The robotic arm plunged down from the ceiling and grabbed hold of William again. It picked him up and moved him through the door. It set him down on the far side and then disappeared back into the first room, and the doors closed with a resounding boom.

William stared at the gigantic room he found himself in now. It looked like a large attic packed to the rafters with tall metal shelves that were crammed full of dust-covered robot parts: arms, legs, hands, and feet. Even heads.

"William?" a familiar voice said.

Benjamin was standing with a group of robots. An old vacuum bot, one he recognized from the dining hall, and two older model guard bots. Relief washed over William. He had made it into the Storeroom for Useless Robots.

"Why did you come in that way?" Benjamin asked. "Through the disinfectant."

"What do you mean?" William asked.

"You could have used the main entrance right there," Benjamin said, pointing to a regular door not far from him. "And where's Max?"

"Max?" William repeated.

"Max was supposed to bring you here."

Now William knew what he was talking about, the argu-bot.

"Um, Max was passivized by some guard bots," William said. "I had to find a different way here on my own."

"Ugh," Benjamin said, clasping his hands together. "That means we don't have much time. They'll be here any minute. Come on."

Benjamin turned and hurried among the shelves, the gang of robots right behind him. A group of the older generation guard bots positioned themselves in front of the door and prepared for an attack.

When William caught up, Benjamin was standing by a large metal table in an open area in the middle of all the shelves. He was surrounded by robots, and they were all looking at William.

"Hi," a voice said.

William spotted Iscia.

"You're here too?" William cried. He was so relieved to see her.

She nodded. "Benjamin got me after what happened down in the lobby. He figured this would be the safest place now. And I got a hologram mask too," she said, holding up a headband.

"Enough chitchat," Benjamin said. "We have important things to deal with."

He waved William over.

There was something sitting on the table that looked like an old architectural blueprint.

"This is the original floorplan for the Institute," Benjamin said. "Here's the main building. This is the park. And these are the ruins of the old castle that once stood here."

Benjamin placed his index finger on the spot where it said *RUINS* in black ink. Next to the ruins it said *PASS-WORD: LOREM IPSUM.*

"What's the password for?" William asked, pointing.

"I'll explain later," Benjamin replied.

William looked over at Iscia. He wondered how much she actually knew about what went on up here in the storeroom.

"This is where it is right now," Benjamin said, tapping his finger on the ruins in the blueprint.

"What is?" William asked.

"The crypto-annihilator," Benjamin said, and looked at William as if he should have already figured out what this was all about.

"And what is that?" Iscia asked.

"It's an advanced code destroyer," Benjamin said. "It's designed to re-scramble difficult codes and destroy them so that they can never be solved. I was tasked with developing it not too long ago. I thought it was supposed to be an experiment, and never imagined that Goffman would actually use it to destroy something as valuable as the code pyramid. I'm afraid my invention may cause quite a lot of damage. Right now I feel like Oppenheimer must have felt after he invented the bomb. Stupid!"

Benjamin shook his head.

"When the alarm went off at Big Ben and the Orbulator Agent resurfaced with the code pyramid, Goffman took the annihilator away from me. I knew I had to get it back, which is why I went into hiding. He's planning to use the crypto-annihilator to destroy the code pyramid."

Benjamin stood there for a moment staring at William.

"I don't have proof, but I fear the worst. There are forces here at the Institute that will do anything to stop you from solving the code and accessing what's inside the code pyramid."

"And what's inside?" Iscia asked.

"The only thing that can stop Abraham Talley when he returns to earth," Benjamin said.

"What is it?" Iscia asked again. It was easy to see that she was getting impatient.

Benjamin shot a quick glance over at William. Like he didn't want to tell them.

"What's inside?" William demanded.

"Antiluridium," Benjamin said finally. "I don't have time to go into detail right now. It will have to wait until later."

Antiluridium. William didn't like the sound of that.

"And these forces within the Institute, that want to stop us from getting at the antiluridium . . . ," William said with a frown. "Are you talking about Goffman?"

"Goffman hasn't been the same since he came back from the Crypto Portal," Benjamin continued. "And a number of people at the Institute have supported him. The alarm at Big Ben and the Orbulator Agent suddenly entering the scene don't help matters."

The robots around them muttered anxiously.

William's thoughts were racing.

Could he trust Benjamin? With his shaggy hair and nervous tics, Benjamin seemed almost crazier than Goffman.

"So the crypto-annihilator is here." Benjamin put his finger on the blueprint again. "In a secret chamber deep beneath the ruins. And soon someone is going to use my invention to try to annihilate the code pyramid that Goffman took from you."

"And—if they manage to annihilate it—then we'll never get to the antiluridium . . . ?" William said haltingly. "And we have nothing to fight Abraham?"

Benjamin nodded.

"The Orbulator Agent gave the pyramid to me," William said. "If only I'd solved it right away, none of this would have happened."

"Don't be so sure," Benjamin mumbled. "It was actually good that you waited to solve it."

"Why?" William asked.

"In the Orbulator Parchment it says . . . ," Benjamin began, then paused to clear his throat. He swallowed, apparently reluctant to finish. "That anyone who attempts to solve the code but fails will . . . die."

A cold silence settled over the small group.

"Does that mean," William said, "that if I had tried to solve it at school but not succeeded, then the pyramid—the orbulator, whatever it's called—would have killed me?"

"Yes, if we're to believe what it says in the Orbulator Parchment," Benjamin said.

He paused and looked out at those assembled.

"The most important thing right now is that we get down to the ruins and stop Goffman from destroying the pyramid. It'll be hard, but I think there are enough of us to do it. . . . I hope so anyway."

"Long live the revolution!" cried one of the robots, raising its hand in the air.

"LONG LIVE THE REVOLUTION," the other robots cried out in unison.

"LONG LIVE—" *ZONK!* One of the robots was hit by a ray of blue light and crashed to the floor in a tremendous cloud of sparks.

William turned around and spotted a group of new guard bots rolling toward them. Every one of them was armed with a passivator.

17

"Iscia, William, run!" Benjamin yelled. "They mustn't catch you. We'll stall them."

William grabbed Iscia and pulled her along with him.

They ran into the stacks, away from the guard bots, then flung themselves behind an overstuffed shelf. William poked his head up and saw how the new guard bots, with their passivators drawn, had already surrounded Benjamin and the little group of retired robots.

"I don't think they noticed us," Iscia whispered.

"Let's hope not," William whispered back.

"What do we do now?"

"I have to get down to the ruins and get that pyramid."

"What do you mean 'I'?"

"You heard what Benjamin said." William gave Iscia a somber look. "It's dangerous."

"You'll never make it on your own. I'm going with you," Iscia said, sounding irritated.

"I don't think so," a hollow voice said from behind them.

They turned around and saw a white guard bot pointing a brand-new passivator right at them.

"Get up!" it commanded.

They stood slowly. William looked around for something he could use as a weapon. His eyes stopped on a big crate filled with round balls that looked like robot eyes. But what was he going to do? Throw eyes at the guard bots? He dismissed the idea.

"Over with the others," the guard bot said, impatiently waving its passivator.

William gestured to Iscia to do as the guard bot said. They walked back over to Benjamin and the other robots.

"Some revolution," one of the white guard bots sniggered.

"What kind of revolution are you guys actually planning up here?" one of the other guard bots asked.

"It's more of a renovation, actually," Benjamin said, maintaining a straight face.

"A renovation?" the guard bot repeated. "What kind of renovation?"

"A renovation . . . of your metal face," Benjamin said,

whacking the robot in the face with a spare robotic leg that he'd had hidden behind his back.

CLANK! went the leg as it hit the guard bot's head. The guard bot staggered backward and toppled over. The other guard bots stood staring at it as it lay motionless on the floor.

"That's all it takes to knock us out of commission?" one of them said, looking to the others.

"Of course," Benjamin said. "I'm the one who built you. You can't withstand very much at all."

The guard bots exchanged glances.

"LET THE REVOLUTION BEGIN!" Benjamin yelled, brandishing the robot leg over his head.

"Finally," a deep voice said from somewhere in the shelves.

William turned. At first he saw only scrap metal, but then he realized that something was moving. An enormous metallic robot came into view. It was three times Benjamin's height.

William gasped.

All the shelves began rattling and clanking as one robot after another crawled and rolled out. Soon there were ten enormous robots around them. They looked like they'd been put together out of miscellaneous scrap parts.

"Finally! Come on, clatter bots!" Benjamin cried.

The guard bots couldn't have been more paralyzed if they'd been passivized. They didn't know what to do now that they were surrounded by gigantic robots on all sides.

Suddenly one of the clatter bots let out a war whoop and, with its arms raised, ran at the guard bots screaming, "ATAAAACK!"

The floor shook as the other clatter bots followed, all yelling in unison.

The guard bots responded by frantically firing their passivators. But for each robot they managed to passivize, two new ones came tumbling out of the overfilled storeroom shelves.

It was chaos. William and Iscia seized their chance to get away. They cautiously snuck backward, into the darkness between the shelves.

They stopped by the opening in the wall where William had entered the room. It was closed now. The terrific clanking commotion from the battle resounded through the vast storeroom. It didn't seem like anyone was following them.

"This is where I came in," William said.

"How do we open it?" Iscia asked, running her hand over the wall.

"No idea. Benjamin mentioned another door in here." William looked around.

There was a sudden ping from somewhere in the room, followed by an electric hum.

William just had time to pull Iscia behind a shelf before a new swarm of guard bots rolled past them.

They waited for the guard bots to pass. Then they set off running until they saw an elevator door that was just sliding shut.

William grabbed the first, best thing he found on a nearby shelf and picked up his pace even more. He had to stop that door from shutting all the way. As he ran, he realized that he was holding a round, metallic robot head in his hands.

"What are you doing?" the head asked him, its eyes popping open.

"Sorry," William said. "But you're part of the revolution now."

"Cool," the robot head said.

William slowed, slid down onto one knee, and pulled his arm backward in an arc. Then he launched the head at the elevator like a bowling ball. It howled in fear as it rolled away, until it wedged itself tight in the elevator door. William was right behind it, but the opening wasn't big enough for him to squeeze through. He tried pushing the doors apart.

"Help me," he said through gritted teeth, looking to Iscia, who had caught up. Together they managed to open the door just enough for them to squeeze inside. William bent down and grabbed the robot head, and the elevator door slid shut with a ding.

"I guess you can come," William said, tucking the robot head under his jacket.

"Me too," Iscia said firmly.

18

William and Iscia ran through the dark park behind the Institute.

"This is completely nuts," Iscia whispered. "How are we going to stop the crypto-annihilator from destroying the orbulator pyramid?"

"Dunno, but that's precisely what we have to do," William said, glancing back at the cybernetic garden cage where he'd hidden not so long ago.

There were two guards standing by the cage now. Here and there William could make out the silhouettes of other robots. The garden was full of guards.

To keep from being discovered, they stayed in the shadow of the tall wall that ran along the edge of the park. When William was totally sure no one could see them, he stopped.

"Do you know where the ruins are?" he asked.

"I've never been there," Iscia said. "But I know they're on the other side of the lake at the end of the park." She pointed into the darkness ahead of them. "They're ruins from the medieval castle that used to be here. There are still underground passageways running under parts of the property, but no one's allowed down there."

"Why not?" William asked.

"They're not very stable. They could collapse at any time," Iscia said.

"Sounds like a great place to hide a crypto-annihilator," William said, and kept going.

Soon they were standing on the far side of the lake. The tall wall that marked the end of the park was only a few yards from them. William glanced at the moon, which was just rising.

"We need to find the entrance fast."

"How?" Iscia said, looking around. They were surrounded by old ruins. Big stones lay strewn about, overgrown with moss and covered with grass and bushes.

"It must be nearby," William whispered. He stopped suddenly when he heard footsteps close by.

Two figures came walking toward them. In the darkness it was impossible to see who they were. But as they stepped into the moonlight, William could see that they were two completely identical elderly women. One had a black suit on, the other a lab coat.

William grabbed Iscia and pulled her behind a bush. They crouched there and listened.

The footsteps stopped a little way away. Then came a complaining squeak of metal against metal. It sounded like a door being opened on rusty hinges. The sound sent shivers through William.

When William finally stuck his head out, the women were gone.

"They went in somewhere over there," he whispered, pointing.

He and Iscia crept along the wall until they stopped in front of a mound of stone blocks.

William started searching.

"Here," Iscia whispered, pulling a bush aside.

Behind it was something that looked like a rusty cellar door. William walked over to her.

"No lock," he whispered, "just a handle."

William reached out his hand and felt the handle. It was cold. The hinges complained as he opened the door.

Old, moss-covered stone stairs disappeared into the darkness below. The only thing William and Iscia could hear was the echo of dripping water. And suddenly William felt like he didn't want to go down there. But it was too late to turn back now.

"Someone's coming," Iscia suddenly whispered.

"Come on," William said, putting his foot on the first step.

Iscia followed right behind him.

William closed the iron door, and the moonlight disappeared.

Now they were engulfed by total darkness. William reached his hand out to the side and found the wall. The uneven surface was covered with moss.

"I can't see anything," Iscia whispered from somewhere in the darkness.

William heard someone fumbling with the other side of the iron door. They had to get away from here.

"Come on," he whispered, and felt his way along through the darkness. He could hear Iscia's cautious footsteps behind him.

The iron door screamed like a hoarse monster as it was pulled up. And once again the cold moon shone down on them.

William and Iscia reached the bottom of the stairs and continued down the narrow stone corridor. There was a faint flicker of light here from torches along the wall. The floor was smooth, and the ceiling was constantly dripping.

"We have to hide," William whispered, and spotted a door just then. "In there."

Iscia hurried in, and William slipped in after her. They

pressed themselves against the cold wall and stood there listening to the approaching footsteps.

Three people passed their hiding place. Judging by their height, they were adults. William was sure they were wearing hologram masks, because they all had the same identical elderly woman's head.

When they were far enough away, William peeked out the doorway.

"We have to change our masks to old women," William said. He located the button on the back of his head and started clicking through the different faces. "Tell me when it's her."

A moment later they had both changed heads to the same old woman. It looked really weird.

"Quick. We have to follow them," he whispered, and waved for Iscia to follow. "They seem like they know where they're going."

They snuck after the figures and stopped when they got to the end of the hallway. William leaned forward and peeked around the corner.

The figures had stopped at an old iron door.

One of them raised a hand and knocked. Three short raps, followed by three long ones, then a short, a long, and a short. A small hatch in the door slid to the side, and the same figure mumbled something that William was too far away to hear. The hatch closed, and the iron door made a deep clank before swinging open. Then the figures walked in.

The door closed behind them with a boom.

"Whatever's happening, it's definitely going on in there," William whispered, and hurried down the hallway. He didn't stop until he reached the rusty door.

He raised his hand and knocked using the same signal the figures before them had used.

The little hatch opened.

"Password," a deep voice said from the darkness within.

William and Iscia stood there staring blankly into space. William's mind was racing.

"Password?" the voice said again. More impatiently now.

Then William remembered the drawing Benjamin had shown them and what had been written in ink next to the ruins on the map.

"Lorem ipsum," William said.

The hatch closed again, and the door opened.

19

William stood there staring straight ahead. They were in a room the size of a regular classroom. The walls were made of stone. It was reminiscent of an old dungeon from the Middle Ages.

There were about thirty people in front of them sitting on folding camping chairs, all with that same old woman's head.

A couple of them turned and looked at William and Iscia. They nodded, and William nodded back. At the other end of the room a makeshift stage had been set up, made of wooden pallets. On the stage sat some object that was covered by a white sheet.

"Let's sit down," William whispered, and pointed to some empty chairs in the very back row.

The other people in the room didn't seem to be interested in them. Everyone was watching the stage expectantly.

William stared at the covered object. There was a hum of voices around them.

Suddenly the lights up by the stage flashed on and off three times, and those present shushed one another. A movement behind the stage curtain caught William's attention.

A sinewy hand came out of the gap between the curtains and pulled them aside. Yet another old woman stepped forward. William tried to make himself as small as possible.

"Welcome," the old woman on the stage said. "Let's get going. Before me is the crypto-annihilator, and here, ladies and gentlemen, is what you've been waiting for."

A gasp ran through the room as the woman lifted the metal pyramid from under her cape.

"That's it," William whispered, pointing.

"The Orbulator Agent is back, and he brought with him the code pyramid. The key to the weapon. He also found his chosen one. But I managed to obtain this before William Wenton had a chance to solve it. The parchment tells the truth." The old woman received an enthusiastic ovation.

A shivery feeling spread through William's body as he realized who the woman on the stage was. The long slender figure, the suit. The sinewy hands and fingers. It had to be Fritz Goffman.

The man that William had, up until today, believed to be on his side. The man who had saved William's life numerous times . . . How could he have changed so dramatically? Or had he always been like this . . . evil?

The figure on the stage touched something at the back of her head, and instantly her face changed back to her own. It *was* Fritz Goffman. His hair was combed back, and there was something strange about one of his eyes. His right eye seemed focused and normal, but his left eye was shifty, darting around the room. As if it were looking at something completely different.

"We've been waiting for this for a while," Goffman continued, moving to stand behind the crypto-annihilator. "Finally, we're here. This is the culmination of a process that has been going on here at the Institute. We are under development. For the better. And I—you!—are leading this development." Goffman paused. He stared at the annihilator.

"This is a direct result of the progress that was made in the Crypto Portal." Goffman swallowed. "Esteemed gathering, we are nearing full control."

"Progress?" Iscia whispered. "What is he talking about?"

Goffman looked out at the audience. It was as if he were staring straight at William now.

William stiffened, afraid that Goffman had recognized him, that he and Iscia had been exposed. Or that this was a trap.

"This is a big moment," Goffman continued. "Destroying the orbulator will make us invincible. The other side will stand no chance against the return of the luridium. And very soon we will be able to welcome Abraham Talley back."

William looked at Iscia. Had Goffman totally lost his mind?

Goffman scanned the rest of the assemblage before he made a grand gesture of flinging out his arms and then turned to the machine.

In a quick motion, he yanked the sheet aside. "Let us begin!"

20

On the stage was a humanlike robot. The very sight of it sent shivers down William's spine. The robot hunched over the table like the grim reaper. It sat there with its mechanical arms stretched out and its head drooped forward like a zombie. There was something really menacing about the way it had composed itself.

"Please welcome the crypto-annihilator!" Goffman said, placing the pyramid on a table in front of the robot. Then he leaned forward and pushed something on the robot's back. The robot's head lifted, and its narrow eyes began to glow red as its metallic body twitched.

Everyone in the room stared at the robot. It blinked its eyes a couple of times while the head turned back and forth as if looking at everyone around it.

"Are you ready to begin?" Goffman asked the robot, which nodded in response.

William sat paralyzed, watching as it picked up the pyramid. For a fraction of a second it seemed like the robot looked back at him. As the evil-looking robot turned its head, William spotted something protruding from its neck. He recognized it immediately: his grandfather's thumb drive. Did the drive and all of his grandfather's knowledge about cryptology amp up the robot's analytical capacity?

A red beam shot out of one of the machine's menacing eyes, and it scanned the pyramid. Soon its shiny metal fingers started working, moving the various pieces of the pyramid, as if it were a completely ordinary Rubik's Cube.

William had to do something. And he had to do it now!

Benjamin had been very explicit that they needed to keep the robot from destroying the orbulator. William looked around. Everyone's attention was focused on the robot on the stage.

He suddenly remembered what he had under his jacket: the robot head he'd found in the storeroom. He carefully pulled it out. Its eyes were glowing red.

"Are you ready to help me one more time?" William whispered.

"Everything for the revolution," the robot head whispered back.

"Uh, what are you doing?" Iscia looked at what William was holding in his hands.

"I'm using the head," William whispered back, and stood up.

"William, are you crazy?" was the last thing Iscia managed to say before William raised the robot head and hurled it at the stage as hard as he could.

"VIVA LA REVOLUCIÓN!" the robot head yelled as it sailed through the air and hit the crypto-bot on the stage right in the chest. The head bounced off the massive robot body and rolled across the floor. The crypto-annihilator stopped what it was doing for a split second, then continued twisting and turning the pieces on the pyramid.

Goffman turned and fixed his eyes on William.

"Grab her!" Goffman yelled, pointing to William.

The two closest guard bots rolled toward William with their passivators raised.

William shot a look at the robot onstage. It continued working on the code pyramid like nothing had happened. The guard bots were now only feet away, and there was nowhere William could run.

Suddenly there was a bang and a loud whistling sound up on the stage, and everyone stopped moving. William had heard that sound before.

He looked toward the crypto-bot. It had stopped moving. It held the code pyramid up in front of itself as sparks began spewing out from the pyramid, and it vibrated violently.

"Noooo!" Goffman shouted, and ran toward the crypto-annihilator.

Goffman stopped as a glowing light appeared inside the pyramid. The light grew brighter and brighter, and the whole pyramid seemed to explode with energy. A loud zap shot through the room, followed by a crash. William instinctively turned his head away from the explosion and held both hands up in front of his face.

Then everything went silent.

When William opened his eyes again and looked toward the stage, the crypto-annihilator (or what used to be the crypto-annihilator) wasn't sitting in the chair. A large lump of glowing metal lay on the floor next to the table. A pair of robot legs poked out from the pile. It looked like lava with legs. The pyramid sat on the floor next to it.

"What happened?" Goffman shouted.

"It looks like your plan failed, Goffman," a voice shouted from the crowd.

"VIVA LA REVOLUCIÓN!" another voice yelled. One of the audience members turned off her hologram mask. It was a robot that appeared to be made of scrap parts. It had to be one of Benjamin's clatter bots.

William looked around. Maybe there were others down here too. And sure enough, one by one more of the meeting's attendees stood up and cried out, "VIVA LA REVOLUCIÓN!"

"Meet me by the exit," William said, pushing Iscia toward the door.

"Where are you going?" Iscia asked, holding on to his arm.

"I'm getting the pyramid back!" William pulled free of her grasp and plowed into the fray. He climbed over chair backs on his way toward the stage. All around him clatter bots and brand-new guard bots were at one another's throats.

One of the revolutionary robots right in front of William was hit by a passivator beam and collapsed to the floor. Another beam zapped past his face. William dropped to the floor, crawling forward.

He reached the edge of the stage and cautiously stuck his head up before climbing onto the stage and crawling toward the glowing heap of smoking metal. He reached for the pyramid, but then he heard Goffman's voice behind him.

"Stop!"

William stiffened, waiting to be hit in the back by a passivator ray.

But that didn't happen. Instead, Goffman stepped behind the robot and stared at William for what felt like forever. His one eye was looking to the side. William had seen that before. It looked familiar.

Goffman leaned forward and found the button on the back of William's hologram mask. With a zap a gleam of light shot out before his eyes.

"Would you look at that?" Goffman said. "I figured you'd find a way to get back to the Institute."

William didn't respond. He just couldn't understand what had changed Goffman this way.

A passivator beam strafed Goffman's shoulder, and he staggered backward and stopped for an instant before collapsing. William looked around and spotted Iscia a little way away. She was holding a passivator in her hands.

"Come on!" she yelled.

"Hold on," William shouted back.

He bent down and grabbed the pyramid. He tried to lift it, but it wouldn't budge. Part of it was stuck in the molten metal. William tried again. It was completely stuck.

"Look out," Iscia shouted.

William looked up and spotted two guard bots heading for the stage, both with their passivators aimed at him.

He cast a desperate glance at the pyramid before hurling himself off the stage and racing over to Iscia. Together they dashed for the door at the far end of the room. Empty-handed.

21

William and Iscia stumbled through the cellar door and into the park. A passivator beam shot out of the opening behind them, hitting the iron door. *BAM!* It sounded like someone had struck an enormous gong, alerting the guard bots in the park to the fact that something was going on—and where they should search.

"This way!" William cried out.

They had to find a place to hide. Somewhere they could think, a place where they could plan what to do next. William had been so certain that he would manage to get the orbulator. Now they were going to have to improvise.

They ran into the darkness, zigzagging through large and small bushes.

"There," Iscia said, pointing to a row of tall trees along the dark lake shore.

"Wait," William said, and stopped. They stood listening. The hum of the guard bots grew closer.

William and Iscia continued toward the line of trees, stopping in front of the first one they came to.

Iscia jumped up and grabbed one of the lowest branches and, with an effortless motion, swung herself up so she was sitting on the branch.

"Come on," she said, reaching down for William.

"Where did you learn to do that?" he whispered, and grasped her hand.

"My yard was full of trees when I was little," she whispered back.

William was not as graceful as Iscia, but a few seconds later he was sitting on the branch beside her.

"We need to climb up higher." Iscia started climbing.

She moved upward quickly and silently, twisting like a lizard between the thick branches. William tried to copy her. Climbing trees in the dark was nowhere near as easy as she made it look.

And yet he made his way up, and it wasn't too long before they were both sitting at the top of the tall tree, looking down at the guard bots' red search beams as they hunted for them far below. William looked up. The tree they were sitting in towered over the others, and he could see all the way to the Institute's main building at the opposite end of the park.

The branches and the trunk were much thinner up here, and every slight movement they made caused everything to sway. The branch William was sitting on was no thicker than his wrist. He felt like it might break at any moment.

"What do we do now?" Iscia whispered.

"No idea," William replied.

He looked around for some way to escape but quickly realized that there was nowhere for them to go. The other trees were too far away. And it was too far to jump down. They were trapped. All they could do was wait and hope they wouldn't be discovered.

William realized with horror what it would be like to be passivized while up in a tree. First they would lose all control of their bodies. Then they would tip off the branches and crash to the ground.

"Can you believe Goffman stole the thumb drive to get his hands on the antiluridium?" William whispered.

Iscia shook her head sadly. "I thought he'd changed lately, but he's gone completely crazy. I—"

She was interrupted by a sound from below them.

Two guard bots had stopped at the foot of their tree. Iscia grabbed hold of William's arm. The guard bots' red beams hit the tree and started moving upward.

Higher and higher.

William held his breath as he followed the progress of the beams with his eyes. It was happening fast. They were already halfway up the tree now. William and Iscia were only seconds from being discovered.

Suddenly the sound of a powerful explosion rang out somewhere in the distance. The whole tree shook.

The beams stopped just beneath them.

William spotted a dark column of smoke rising from the roof of the Institute building.

When he looked down again, the red beams were gone, and he heard the guard bots' electric motors humming away from them in the darkness.

William and Iscia sat quietly until they were completely sure the guard bots were gone. They stared at the orange flames flickering out of a big hole in the roof of the main building.

"It looks like something exploded up in the storeroom," Iscia said, her voice fearful.

"Benjamin and the others are up there," William said. And before he was actually aware of what he was doing, he was on his way down the tree trunk. "We have to do something."

It was much faster getting down than it had been climbing up.

William lowered himself from the bottom branch. Iscia landed right next to him. They heard the humming of guard bots moving away from them, toward the main building.

"What in the world is going on?" Iscia asked.

"There's only one way to find out," William said, and started walking toward the Institute.

"Are you crazy?" protested Iscia. "It's crawling with guard bots over there."

"What else are we going to do?" William said, turning to face her. "We have to do something. Benjamin is in there. He needs help."

A few minutes later they were running through the park, heading for the main building.

They slowed down as they approached. The moon was high in the sky, and the cold light reflected off the guard bots assembled on the lawn.

"We have to get past them," William said decisively. He knew he couldn't abandon Benjamin. And he knew what he had to do, even if the thought of it terrified him. It was the only chance they had.

"Wait here until I come back," he told Iscia. "Hide, and don't come out no matter what happens."

"What do you mean?" Iscia asked.

"Just wait here," William urged before he turned and started walking toward the guard bots. "If I'm not back in half an hour, then get out of here."

"But they're going to passivize you" he heard Iscia say from behind him; he kept going anyway.

He stopped a little way from a group of guard bots.

There were more than thirty of them. They all had their backs to him as they peered up at the burning roof. A fire alarm was going off somewhere inside the building.

William looked around and spotted a rock in the flower bed right beside him. He picked it up.

"HEY!" he yelled, and threw the rock as hard as he could at the guard bots.

It hit one of them right on the head with a hollow clank.

They all turned toward him.

The guard bot, which now had a large dent in the back of its head, raised its passivator and fired.

22

William dangled like a rag between two guard bots rolling at top speed down a hallway in the main building.

The fact that they seemed so goal-oriented told William that they knew where to go. And that was exactly what he was counting on: They were taking him straight to Goffman.

William still couldn't move from the passivization. And it seemed like the new passivators did more than just knock out your muscles. His bones all felt like they'd been turned into rubber.

The guard bots braked in front of a door at the end of the hall, and one of them entered a code into the control panel next to the door.

The door opened with a blip.

They emerged into the lobby. Clearly, they had taken one of the secret back entrances.

The lobby was teeming with guard bots. They swarmed back and forth while gazing up at the escalators, which weren't moving. It seemed like they were waiting for something, preparing for something.

William could hear distant rattling and clanking from the floors above. It sounded like a massive orchestra of toddlers heading toward them.

"Why did you bring him here?" a familiar voice yelled.

William was just barely able to look to the side and spotted Goffman, who was pushing his way through the robots toward them. His two red-haired chauffeurs were right behind him.

"But this is William Wenton," one of the guard bots holding William said.

"And he threw a rock at us," another one said. "Very hard."

"At Ted," a third said, pointing to the guard bot standing at the very back, the one with the big dent in his head.

Goffman stopped in front of them, his brow furrowed. He hadn't looked at William yet. His left hand was stuck inside his jacket. It reminded William of the way Napoleon often stood in paintings. It looked strange. Had Goffman injured it?

"Nobody should be in here now. Especially not him."

Goffman pointed to William with his free hand, still without looking at him. "We're in a state of emergency. Only authorized personnel can be in here."

"But he threw a rock . . ."

"SILENCE!" Goffman yelled.

Several of the robots lowered their heads and stared at the floor. As if they were scared to look Goffman in the eye. A dark look had come over his eyes—a darkness William hadn't seen before—and it frightened him.

"Get him out of here," Goffman commanded, and pointed at the door they had just come in through. His left hand was still hidden inside his jacket.

William tried to say something, but his mouth wasn't working. He was dying to confront Goffman, ask why he'd done all this.

"Out!" Goffman yelled, shoving a guard bot so it staggered backward and clanked against the robot behind it. Goffman's body twitched, as if he were having some sort of attack. He grabbed his head.

"Get out of here . . . NOW!" Goffman trembled, and his face contorted with pain. "Nooooo," he said through his teeth.

The guard bots began to wheel back toward the door. William wanted to protest, but he still couldn't make a sound. He tried to squirm and kick his legs to get free, but was only able to flap vaguely a couple of times.

"STOP!" Goffman yelled. "Where are you going?" His voice sounded strangely hoarse and gurgly now, as if he had something stuck in his throat.

The guard bots stopped in their tracks. If anything, they seemed confused by the conflicting orders.

"You just told us we should get out of here," one of the guard bots said without turning around.

"I said no such thing," Goffman barked. His voice was harsh and dry now. "Come back here this instant!"

The guard bots glanced at each other, unsure what to do.

William dangled between them. He tried to turn his head to see behind him, but his body still wouldn't obey.

It was like Goffman suddenly had someone else's voice. It sounded like a combination of Goffman's voice and . . .

William froze. How could that be? She had pulverized herself with her own hand in the Crypto Portal. And why would Goffman talk with her voice?

"You have three seconds," Goffman hissed. "I make metal dust from disobedient robots."

The guard bots turned but remained in place, hesitating. William glanced at Goffman, and now he had no doubt. Somehow or other, Fritz Goffman had Cornelia Strangler's voice.

And for the first time since Goffman had entered the lobby, he pulled his hand out of his jacket. He did it slowly, as if he wanted William to take it in.

It felt like an electric shock had jolted William's body, and he gasped.

Goffman had Cornelia Strangler's hand, the one that had been on display in the glass case.

"You are exactly the boy I've been looking for," Goffman said in Cornelia's hoarse voice, striding toward William. "But that softhearted fool Goffman has been fighting me."

Goffman pushed his way through all the guard bots. It was as if he were moving in slow motion. The mood in the lobby had changed completely. The entire space had gone quiet, and the air had gotten colder.

Goffman stopped right in front of William and stood there staring at him before leaning forward. And now William smelled it, the same stench that had always followed Cornelia: the odor of burned rubber.

"You're an interesting fellow, huh?" Goffman whispered in Cornelia's hoarse voice. "I could have used someone like you, but Goffman says you're not worth having."

William didn't respond.

His eyes were riveted on that mechanical hand.

A new explosion came from somewhere above them. The floor shook, and the metal bodies of all the robots in the lobby clanged as they banged into one another.

Goffman jumped, and his face contorted in pain.

"They're coming," Goffman said in his normal voice,

looking up at the escalators. Then he turned to William, grabbing his collar and pulling him close. "William, get out of here. She's inside of me. And there's nothing I can do to stop her. You need to run."

Goffman's body twitched again, and his eyes turned black.

"What's the hurry, you little brat?" he growled hoarsely with Cornelia's voice. "Let's give *him* the pyramid . . . let *him* destroy it."

Yet again Goffman's body twitched.

"This little rodent will have to destroy it himself. What a sweet irony."

Goffman nodded to one of the chauffeurs, who walked over to them, opened a leather bag, and pulled out the pyramid. Somehow they had retrieved it from the molten crypto-annihilator.

Goffman turned to William and held the pyramid up in front of him.

Yet another explosion shook the building. Little chunks of concrete came loose from the ceiling and rained down on the guard bots. It sounded like hail on a tin roof.

"You'd better hurry!" Goffman barked with Cornelia's voice, shoving the pyramid into William's limp hands. "If you don't destroy it, there's no need for you anymore." Goffman made a cutting gesture with his hand over his throat.

"No." The word suddenly slipped out of William's mouth. He was as surprised as the others that he could talk again. The passivization was wearing off, and he was able to move his head.

"What did you say?" Goffman said. If possible, his eyes grew even darker. His left eye popped out to the side just like Cornelia's eye had done. He took a menacing step toward William, pointing at him with the mechanical hand.

"I'm not going to destroy it," William said decisively. "I will never do it!"

"I have a better idea," Goffman said, and pointed to one of the chauffeurs. "Bring him in here."

The chauffeur raised a small walkie-talkie and muttered something into it.

A few seconds later, one of the doors to the lobby opened, and two guard bots rolled in with Benjamin drooping between them.

23

A new explosion boomed above them. Large cracks had formed in the concrete of the ceiling. It seemed as if the entire Institute building was crumbling.

"Don't do as he says," Benjamin yelled when he spotted William. "Don't do it! No matter what he threatens!"

The guard bots carrying Benjamin stopped beside Goffman.

"Now, William," he said. "Shall I show you what I do with mutineers?"

He nodded to one of the guard bots, which raised its free arm. In its hand it held something that looked like a long pipe, but on the side of the pipe there were several glowing joysticks and buttons. The guard bot aimed the pipe at Benjamin and pushed a couple of the buttons.

Benjamin started floating. It must have been some sort of antigravitation modulator. He flew upward and didn't stop until he hung just below the ceiling, nearly thirty feet above them. Only now did William notice how many cracks there actually were up there. The explosions were destroying the whole building.

"Don't let him threaten you into destroying it," Benjamin yelled. "We need that pyramid!"

Goffman aimed his mechanical hand at Benjamin and began fiddling with the buttons.

"Silence," he commanded.

"William . . . ," Benjamin began. But he didn't get to say anything more before a blue beam hit him in the shoulder. Benjamin flopped over in midair but remained hanging there.

"There," Goffman said, and turned to face William. "Benjamin has always been a little too chatty. And so have you."

Goffman pointed the hand at William.

"You should have left when you had the chance," he said. "There's really no use for you here."

William froze. Was Goffman really about to zap him? He shut his eyes and felt his body tense.

There was an audible crash from somewhere or other in the Institute. William opened his eyes as a handful of guard bots jumped to the side just as a large block of concrete came loose from the ceiling and thundered to the floor.

Still pointing the hand at William, Goffman looked up at the ceiling.

"What's going on?" he mumbled.

Clattering sounds could be heard from the floor above them. Hundreds of wheels squeaking and metallic feet running.

The guard bots lined up in a row and pointed their passivators at the escalators in the middle of the hall.

The clattering stopped, and the lobby grew totally silent. William glanced over at Goffman. He stood just as still as the guard bots, eyes fixed on the top of the stairs. For a moment it seemed like he had forgotten William. Instead, he was pushing some buttons on the mechanical hand so it started beeping. William knew what that meant. Goffman was getting ready to use it.

Something moving at the top of the stairs caught William's attention. A figure came into view.

It was the argu-bot.

Suddenly William realized what was happening. The retired robots had managed to overpower the guard bots up in the attic.

The revolution was underway.

Goffman showed no sign of backing down. He was surrounded by several hundred guard bots. There was only one way this could go.

"I'll give you one chance to go back where you came

from unharmed," Goffman yelled in an authoritative voice, aiming his mechanical hand at them.

"I think you're full of horse manure!" the argu-bot shouted back.

"I'll show you horse manure!" Goffman raised the hand and fired off a blue beam. The beam hit a column just above the argu-bot, and blue sparks rained down.

"Attack!" the argu-bot cried out, and then raced down the escalator.

"Down with Goffman!" a sea of different voices exclaimed, and William gasped as a wave of robots somehow clattered down the escalators. There were hundreds of them, swarming like angry ants.

The guard bots in the lobby shot one salvo after another at the clatter bots. They tumbled down the stairs. On the way down they crashed into the guard bots and drowned them in an avalanche of metal. But no matter how many clatter bots the guard bots managed to shoot, new ones appeared in an endless stream of metal bodies in all shapes and forms.

William looked down at the pyramid in his hands.

He turned his head and glanced at the door behind him. This was his chance.

"Get him!" Goffman yelled from somewhere in the racket.

William spotted Goffman a little way off. The tall man

towered over the robots and was pointing his mechanical hand directly at William.

"Get that little rodent!" Goffman shouted.

A handful of guard bots immediately followed the order.

William tightened his grip on the pyramid. He turned and started running for the door.

Behind him he could hear Goffman's hoarse cry: "Stop him! He can't get away with the orbulator!"

Three guard bots turned toward William, and he knew he wasn't going to be able to escape. But then a figure tackled the guard bots. It rolled into one of the guard bots and hit it hard, and then hit another in the head with the back end of a passivator. The figure turned toward William. It was Iscia.

"It died on me," she shouted, and held up the passivator. "But it's still good for a club. Come on—let's get out of here!"

She motioned for him to follow as she ran toward the door.

William and Iscia raced out into the park behind the Institute and kept going into the darkness. The sound of the robot battle faded and disappeared behind them.

24

William and Iscia ran through the woods behind the Institute.
It had been surprisingly easy to get over the fence at the
end of the park. True, it was high, but it was easy to climb,
and they hadn't seen or heard a single guard bot. They were
probably all inside the main building, where the action was.
And the action was exactly what William and Iscia wanted
to get as far away from as possible right now.

When their feet hit the ground on the other side of
the fence, William felt a sense of relief surge through his
body.

"This way," Iscia whispered, and continued into the
dark woods.

William set off after her. He looked back over his shoulder as he ran, but all he could see were the trees standing

like tall skeletons in the moonlight. Had they really managed to escape with the pyramid?

Iscia stopped. She stood there, looking around while she gasped for breath. Her face was drenched with sweat. "Did you hear that?"

"What?" William said under his breath.

"Sounded like an engine," Iscia said, looking up at the night sky.

"If it came from up there," William said, "it might be a drone. We have to find somewhere to hide."

William's hands were so clammy he was having trouble holding the smooth metal pyramid. He stuck it under his sweater and hoped it wouldn't start sparking. After having seen what the pyramid did to the crypto-annihilator, he was much more apprehensive about the thing.

They peered around warily, trying to make out anything among the trees in the darkness. But it was completely still now.

"Look," Iscia said, pointing at something in between the dark trees. "Looks like some kind of shed. Come on!"

"It's a bunker," William whispered as they came closer.

In front of them was a partially collapsed concrete bunker. It was hidden behind a rotting tree. The roof had caved in a long time ago, and only the walls remained.

"We can hide in there until we're sure no one is following us." They walked through the low doorway together.

The room was small, and the floor was covered with broken glass and other trash.

"It's dry over here," Iscia said from behind him.

She sat down on a solid piece of concrete that had at one time been part of the roof.

William flopped down beside her.

They sat in total silence for a while, listening to the trees rustling against one another in the breeze. William looked up at the starry sky above. He thought back to the wheat field back home in Norway, and how they'd been caught by one of Goffman's drones.

As he sat there, looking up at the sky, he thought for a moment that he heard the distant hum of a motor. Or maybe it was his imagination playing tricks on him.

"What happened in there?" Iscia asked.

William looked at Iscia.

"She's back," he whispered. It felt strange saying it out loud like that.

"Who is?" Iscia said.

"Cornelia," William said. His voice was trembling. It was like he could still smell that burned stench that always followed her.

The color drained from Iscia's face.

"Cornelia Strangler?" she asked.

William only nodded in reply.

"How?"

"She's inside Goffman's head," William said. "She came from the hand."

Iscia sat silently for a while. William could see that her brain was working on overdrive now.

"Was that why she zapped herself in the Himalayas?" she finally said.

And now William understood what she was thinking.

"She defragmented herself and somehow stored herself inside the hand," William said.

"And Goffman brought the hand back to the Institute," Iscia added. "And probably tried it on, and that was it."

"How could he have been so stupid?" William said, and shook his head. "He knows how dangerous that mechanical hand is."

"Maybe she did the same thing to him as she did to Freddy," Iscia said. "She could telepathically make people do stuff. Remember?"

William nodded solemnly. How could he forget how Freddy had followed Abraham Talley into the Crypto Portal? It seemed like someone else had taken control of his body, forcing him to go into the portal. It had to have been Cornelia.

"She's dead set on destroying this." William pulled out the pyramid. He sat there for a couple of seconds, looking at the strange symbols on the surface of the ancient pyramid.

"I have to solve it," he said without taking his eyes off

the pyramid. "That's the only thing that can stop all this. I have to solve it *now*!"

"Are you crazy?" Iscia blurted out. "You saw what happened to that crypto-annihilator! It melted. And so will you if you don't make it."

"You don't think I can do it?" William looked up at her.

"I don't know," Iscia said. "Maybe it's the hardest code in the universe. Maybe it's completely impossible. Or maybe it's a trap. What if this is exactly what they want, for you to solve it and get yourself killed in the process?"

William looked down at the pyramid again. Felt the surface. Pictured in his mind how it had glowed before it destroyed the crypto-annihilator. He felt fear surging through his body. Suddenly solving the pyramid didn't seem like a good idea anymore.

"Let's keep going." Iscia got up.

But William didn't move. He couldn't take his eyes off the pyramid. Should he let the fear decide for him? What kind of code breaker was he if he let the fear of what might happen stop him?

"I have no choice," he whispered.

"What do you mean, *no choice*?" Iscia looked at him in horror.

"I have to solve the pyramid. As long as I have it, Cornelia will keep looking for us."

"No!" Iscia exclaimed. "You could die! We have to find another solution. We can leave it here and just go."

In the moonlight, William saw that Iscia's eyes had welled up with tears. He took a deep breath.

"There's no other solution, Iscia," he said. "I have to."

She stood there for something that felt like forever, just staring at him. Then she sat back down again.

"You'd better make it!" she whispered.

"If something goes wrong," William said, "you have to get out of here—promise me!"

She gave him a quick nod.

"Promise," William urged.

"Promise," she said.

William was glad she was staying. She was a true friend. He focused on the pyramid, then closed his eyes.

The vibrations began right away, meaning that this was a powerful code.

William hesitated. He let go of the pyramid with one hand and balanced it on his lap with the other. The vibrations stopped halfway up his spine, hovering there.

It wasn't too late to quit. He could leave the pyramid in the bunker, do what Iscia said. Someone would find it; then it would be *their* problem.

No!

The Orbulator Agent had given it to him specifically. It was his problem, and he would deal with it. Besides, William couldn't risk Goffman getting it again. William had to solve it. Now!

Once again, William grabbed the pyramid with both hands. He concentrated on the vibrations. They moved up his spine and out into his arms, hands, and fingers.

He opened his eyes. The pyramid was glowing. All the strange symbols pulsed with a golden light as they swirled around in the air above him. Only William could see this. This was how the luridium in his body helped him crack codes.

William focused on the floating symbols, and they started to form complex patterns. They were fast. William needed to be fast too.

Based on the symbols' formations, William was able to calculate how to twist the various parts of the pyramid. He turned the first part and heard a low, satisfying click. And one by one the parts ticked into place. Images of how the pyramid had started to glow before destroying the crypto-annihilator flashed in front of William's eyes. He wanted to stop but knew that he couldn't. The vibrations had really grabbed hold of him now. It was too late to turn back. His fingers continued working. His only concern was to not fail.

If he did, he would be dead in a flash.

He knew that Iscia was still sitting next to him. He could barely see her in his peripheral vision. If things didn't go as planned, he only wished that she had the sense to get out of there so that the pyramid wouldn't destroy them both.

William continued working as the strange glowing symbols swirled around him. This code was taking longer than usual to solve. It was a difficult code.

Then suddenly the vibrations vanished. So did the glowing symbols.

William was left sitting there in the dark with the metallic pyramid in his hand. Had he solved it?

"Are you done?" Iscia asked from somewhere in the darkness.

"I don't know," William said without taking his eyes off the pyramid.

Had he done it?

He wasn't sure. But he was still alive.

"I hear something. There's someone out there in the woods," Iscia whispered. "We have to get out of here."

Suddenly the pyramid started vibrating. William let go of it, and it toppled onto the ground. The vibrations grew stronger. And the pyramid emitted a high-frequency sound.

"What's going on?" Iscia said.

"I don't know," William replied.

Did this mean that he hadn't actually cracked the code, and that the pyramid was preparing to kill him?

"William," Iscia whispered. "We have to go. Someone's coming!"

Suddenly the pyramid levitated, stopping right in front

of William's face. William wanted to run, but his muscles wouldn't obey him. He stared at the hovering pyramid. Then the inside of the pyramid lit up, and a beam of light shot out of it, rising into the night sky like an enormous beacon.

"William!" Iscia sounded really scared now. "We have to go." She pulled at his arm.

The pyramid turned and shot out the door.

William and Iscia stumbled after it.

25

"There it is," William said, and pointed at the light in the dark woods. "We have to follow it."

William and Iscia ran after the levitating pyramid.

"There's someone after us," Iscia said just as a blue passivator ray hit one of the trees next to them. "Guard bots!"

William turned and saw the dark silhouettes of two robots coming toward them.

"Come on," he said, hurrying after the floating pyramid.

William ran onto a road that cut through the woods and came to a sudden stop as two bright lights blinded him.

"Watch out!" Iscia was right behind him.

William flung himself to the side just as a large semi-trailer whizzed past at tremendous speed. It careened all over the road, seemingly trying to regain control. It had changed lanes, obviously to prevent a collision with something on the road. William and Iscia stood there watching its red taillights disappear into the darkness.

"There!" Iscia said, and pointed. "The pyramid."

And there it was. It hovered in the middle of the road. The beam of light was still shining into the sky and bathed the area in brightness.

"Can't you turn that thing off?" Iscia asked. "They're going to find us."

"I don't think there's anything I can do," William said, and moved closer to the pyramid. He stopped and followed the beam up into the sky with his eyes. "It's like a beacon," he whispered.

"Exactly," Iscia said. "And the guard bots will find us." She pulled off her jacket and placed it over the pyramid. The beam of light vanished.

"There," she said with a relieved smile.

They stood there for a few seconds staring at Iscia's jacket, which hovered in midair. The bright light from the pyramid glowed from inside.

"This is definitely the main road," Iscia said. "Maybe we can get a ride?"

"As in hitchhike?" William stared at her. "No one hitchhikes anymore. . . ."

"Well, how else are we going to get out of here?" she said.

"Is that what we're doing?" William stared at Iscia. "Getting out of here? What about Benjamin, and this thing?" He pointed at the hovering pyramid.

Iscia didn't respond. Her eyes radiated frustration.

Suddenly she startled and looked around.

"Do you hear that?" Iscia stared into the darkness.

"What?" William couldn't hear anything other than the whispering of the trees in the woods.

"That hum?"

Now William heard it too. It was the same noise they had heard when they were hiding in the bunker. Only now it was coming closer.

Then he spotted a powerful light behind the dark treetops. It seemed to be heading straight for them.

"Is that a drone?" William whispered. "We have to get out of here."

"That's no drone," Iscia said. "It's a plane."

William squinted at the sky. She was right.

It was an old propeller plane, painted bright red.

They stared at the little plane as it descended toward the road where they were standing.

"Looks like it's going to land," William said.

"Here?" Iscia sounded scared.

"Come on!" Together they hid behind a large bush along the shoulder of the road.

They listened to the approaching propeller.

There was a squeal of rubber as the tires hit the asphalt.

The engine sputtered and coughed, and then there was a sudden loud bang.

"Well, it's not from the Institute, anyway," William said. "They don't have a plane that old."

The plane stopped right by the bush William and Iscia were hiding behind.

The engine spluttered a couple more times before going quiet.

"Well, are you planning on spending the whole night back there or what?" a voice suddenly asked. "We really ought to get going."

William and Iscia remained quiet as mice.

"I'm on my way to London," the voice continued. "And I have room . . ."

William and Iscia looked at each other but didn't move.

"Fine, fine . . . ," the voice said. "It's up to you. Anyway, I offered. I asked you to dance, and you turned me down."

There was something familiar about that voice. William was sure he'd heard it before.

And before he had time to change his mind, he peeked out of his hiding place.

The plane was parked in the middle of the road. It was an old Spitfire from the Second World War. William knew the make because he'd seen pictures of planes like this. It looked like a shark with wings.

A man in a leather hat and earmuffs sat at the controls. He slid his round aviator's goggles up onto the top of his head.

William recognized him right away.

It was the same man who'd given him the pyramid outside his house in Norway. It was the mailman. Or the Orbulator Agent, as Benjamin had called him. Although now he looked like a World War II pilot.

"I see that you finally solved it," the pilot said, and motioned toward the hovering pyramid. "Would you mind bringing it over here? I would do it myself, but my legs are stiff from all the sitting."

William hesitated.

"Do as he says," Iscia whispered, and poked William in the back. "Give it to him."

"How?" William said.

"Just give it a push," the pilot said. "Like you'd push a car."

Carefully William walked over to the floating pyramid. He stopped next to it and poked it with his finger. It wobbled a little.

"Come on," the pilot said impatiently. "We don't have all day!"

William put both hands on the pyramid and pushed. It responded by floating willingly toward the old plane.

Soon it bumped gently into the side of the plane. The pilot reached for it and pulled Iscia's jacket off.

"Whose jacket is this?" he said, holding it up.

"Mine," Iscia said, coming out from behind the bush.

"Catch," the pilot said, and threw the jacket toward her. She caught it and put it on.

The pilot grabbed the pyramid and placed it on his lap. He turned it a couple of times, and the light turned off.

"Jump in," he said, and waved at them. "We're in a hurry."

William and Iscia looked at each other. Was it safe?

Suddenly they heard the unmistakable sound of guard bots crashing through the woods.

Without another thought, William ran over to the old plane. Iscia followed him.

"On board, you two," the Orbulator Agent said.

William and Iscia climbed up onto the wing and then tumbled in behind the pilot's seat. William looked toward the two guard bots. They had their passivators raised, ready to shoot.

"Hold on tight. Let the dance begin." The Orbulator Agent pushed in a button on the control panel. The powerful engine started, and the propeller began to spin. The plane gathered momentum moving down the road, and William and Iscia were pressed against the seat back.

The plane roared down the road and then took off.

It went fast, very fast. William felt his stomach tickle. The wind tugged at his hair, and he realized he was freezing.

Soon they were high above the treetops. William looked at the guard bots on the road far below.

"We did it!" he cheered.

★ ★ ★

The man who had saved William and Iscia, the Orbulator Agent, sat in the pilot's seat in front of them. William studied him from behind as best he could. The skin on his face was very pale, almost white. And now he noticed something else. His skin seemed as if it were composed of smaller pieces, like a puzzle. He was neatly dressed in an old suit, and over his suit he wore a coat with large, bulging pockets. In fact, they were crammed full of things. William even thought he saw a small, black London taxi poking out of one.

"How did you know we were behind those bushes?" William asked.

"You solved the orbulator," the Orbulator Agent said.

"And you saw the beam of light," Iscia said.

"Yes. I've been in the area, waiting for that to happen."

William and Iscia exchanged looks. This man was really odd.

"Where in London are you going?" William asked.

"I'm going where you're going," the Orbulator Agent responded.

"And where is that?" William inquired.

"The first stop is Big Ben. Let's tango."

The plane changed direction and proceeded upward through the dense cloud layer.

26

The old plane putted along under the clear night sky. William couldn't see the ground. It was completely hidden by the clouds below them. He just had to trust that they really were on their way to London.

He didn't want to think about how high up they were now. Especially since it sounded like the old plane's engine might cut out any minute. Every now and then it backfired with a loud *bang!* and then went completely silent—before coming back to life again.

The cold wind hit William's face, and he'd already lost the feeling in his fingers. He pulled his jacket even tighter around himself and huddled in the seat in an attempt to get out of the wind a little.

Iscia looked cold too. Her face had lost all its color. Her

thin windbreaker wasn't much help against the freezing winds at this altitude.

The pilot had been sitting silently with his back to them for the last half hour.

William cautiously leaned closer to Iscia. "Do you think we can trust him?" he whispered.

Iscia shrugged. "Don't know," she replied. "I'm too cold to think right now!"

"I'm sure you two have a bunch of questions," the pilot called back to them, and suddenly let go of the control stick and leaped around. He was squatting on the front seat and staring at them.

"Shouldn't you be flying the plane?" William exclaimed, pointing at the controls.

"Relax." The pilot smiled proudly. "Even though this plane is old, it has an autopilot. I installed it myself fifty, maybe sixty years ago. I like tinkering with these things. It relaxes me."

The pilot's eyes moved back and forth between William and Iscia. Then it was as if he suddenly realized something.

"You guys are cold," he exclaimed, looking concerned.

"It's fine," Iscia said, her teeth chattering. "We can deal with it."

"Nonsense," the pilot said, and pushed a button on his control panel. "Autopilot wasn't the only thing I installed on this plane."

A panel opened on the front of the plane and a glass roof unfolded and settled down over them. William felt more relaxed the instant the cold wind stopped. He could feel Iscia starting to relax next to him.

The pilot sat there, looking at them. Now and again, slight turbulence made the small plane rattle.

"Are you really the Orbulator Agent?" Iscia asked.

"Oh, sorry," the pilot said. "I see that I forgot to introduce myself in all the excitement. This is a big day. No one has ever solved the pyramid. I can get forgetful on occasions like this."

He held out his hand and greeted first Iscia, then William. His hand was neither cold nor warm, just completely neutral. On it, too, his skin was like puzzle pieces.

"My name is Philip," he said. "But I prefer Phil. And, yes, I am what they like to call the Orbulator Agent. But I don't use that title very often. It's too formal. Makes me sound like a tax collector or the foreign minister."

"But what is it that you do?" William asked.

"A very good question," Phil said, smiling. "I am so old that I've almost forgotten myself. My main job is to give the code pyramid—the orbulator—to the person who can solve the code."

"And this orbulator," Iscia said. "Is that a weapon?"

"Very much so, indeed!" A huge grin shot across Phil's pale face. "A very powerful weapon. Very, very powerful."

"So now," Iscia continued, "you're going to give this weapon to William?"

Phil looked at William affectionately.

"You wouldn't believe how long I've waited for someone like you to come along," he said with a trembling voice. "I just knew you would solve the first code."

"First code?" William gasped. "What do you mean?"

"I'll tell you more about that later. First we have to get to Londinium."

"Londinium?" Iscia repeated. "You mean London?"

"Sorry," Phil said, shaking his head in embarrassment. "I mean London, of course. Haven't really gotten used to the new name yet. Londinium is what the Romans used to call it back in the day."

"What are we going to do when we get to London?" William asked.

Phil leaned toward them and looked around before folding his hands in front of him.

"I've been waiting for this for a long time," he whispered. "Sorry if I seem a little stunned. This is really big for me. I had given up hope, actually."

William stared at Phil.

"Well." Phil looked up at the sky, as if he had to really think about what he was going to tell them. "What was the question you asked?"

"Why are we going to London?" William asked.

"Londinium is the first stop on the way to the weapon," Phil said.

"The first stop?" William said.

"Yes." Phil nodded. "I need to take care of some stuff there." Phil did a quick little wave with his hand as if these were unimportant details. "Think of Londinium as a stop-over on the way to our destination."

"A stopover? Is it far to where we're going? Where is this weapon anyway?"

"The Mariana Trench," Phil said as if he were talking about somewhere just down the street. "If you want to hide something, the Mariana Trench is the perfect place to do it."

William and Iscia looked at each other. The Mariana Trench was on the other side of the world. It was the deepest place on the earth and, as a result, mostly unexplored. A perfect place to hide things, and for that very same reason, probably a terrible place to get to.

"Are we losing altitude?" Iscia asked, looking around. The small plane shook as they hit a layer of thick, gray clouds.

William peered out the window and grabbed hold of his seat.

"Whoops!" Phil turned around and grabbed the control stick with both hands. "It just occurred to me that it was one of the other planes I put the autopilot in. This plane doesn't fly itself. I really am starting to get old."

Phil pulled the control stick toward himself hard, and the plane tipped up and started climbing again.

William sat there in silence. He was thinking about what Phil had said. Were they really going to the Mariana Trench?

27

"William!"

William opened his eyes and looked around. He was still sitting in the plane, but he must have dozed off.

Iscia was shaking him.

"Look!" She pointed out at the ground below. "We're there."

William rubbed his eyes, pressed his face to the window, and looked down. He beheld a sea of little twinkling lights in all the colors of the rainbow.

"Isn't it beautiful?" Iscia sighed in delight.

William nodded. "There's a landing strip," he said, pointing. "That must be where we're going." He sat back in the seat and tightened his seat belt.

They waited.

"We're flying past it?" Iscia pointed to the airstrip as they passed over it.

"Aren't we going to land?" William poked Phil on the shoulder, but Phil didn't respond.

"Phil?" William tried again. "Philip?" He tapped his shoulder again, harder this time. "Orbulator Agent?"

No reaction.

Iscia undid her seat belt and leaned forward to look at Phil.

"His eyes are closed," she said.

"Closed?" William said. "He can't land the plane with his eyes closed, can he?"

"Phil?" Iscia shook him. *"Phil?"* she shouted, and slapped his face.

"What is it?" Phil yelled, his eyes opening wide. "Run! The dinosaurs are coming!" He stared at Iscia, as if he couldn't place her. Then he smiled broadly.

"Did you have a nice trip? Sometimes a nap is just the thing. That's something I started doing back in the Dark Ages. I don't actually need to nap, mind you, but by now it's become something of a habit."

"We're going to crash!" Iscia yelled.

"Apparently." Phil looked at the lights below them. Then he grabbed the control stick with both hands and turned the plane around.

"This is the perfect place to land," he said, pointing to a large, dark patch on the ground ahead of them.

"What is it?" Iscia asked.

"Hyde Park," Phil responded, pushing the control stick forward.

The nose of the plane was pointed at the ground. The body of the plane started shaking so strongly that William was scared the whole thing would fall apart.

They were heading for some tall treetops. The plane kept going, into the trees. Branches were slapping the wings. It seemed as if it was totally out of control. This might turn out to be the end of both this London trip . . . and them.

The wheels hit the ground with a loud bump, and gradually the plane came to a stop with its nose planted deep inside a large bush. Phil unbuckled his seat belt and pushed a button on the control panel. The glass roof disappeared into the panel on the nose again.

"Welcome to Londinium!" Phil jumped out of the plane and down to the ground.

William and Iscia followed and looked around. It was the middle of the night, and there wasn't a soul about.

"We ought to get out of here," Phil said. "They don't like people landing in the park." He thrust his hand into one of the big pockets in his jacket and pulled out something that looked like an old TV remote.

He aimed it at the plane and pushed one of the buttons.

With a loud zap and a bright flash of light the plane was gone.

"Where did it go?" Iscia blurted out.

"There," William said, pointing to something on the ground where the plane had been.

"Wow!" Iscia exclaimed. "Coooool!"

The plane hadn't disappeared. It was still there. But it was smaller, a lot smaller. It was no bigger than a toy now.

Phil strode over to the little plane, picked it up, and stuck it in one of his jacket pockets. From one of his other pockets he pulled out a little green military tank. He studied it in the light from a lamppost.

"No," he mumbled in irritation. "That won't do." He put it back in his pocket and pulled out a small locomotive.

"Where did it go?" he said, returning the locomotive to his pocket.

He tried yet another pocket and pulled out a small black car.

"There you are," he said with satisfaction, and set the car down on the grass.

He took a couple of steps back. "It'd be wise to back up a bit," he said. "Sometimes they just explode."

He pointed the remote at the car and pushed a button.

With another zap the small black car suddenly became a full-size London taxicab.

"How do you do that?" William asked.

"Molecular shrinkology," Phil said, and stuffed the remote into his pants pocket. He did a little jump, danced over to the cab, and opened one of the back doors. "Get in," he sang.

★ ★ ★

William and Iscia clung tightly to the backseat as the cab sped through the streets.

"Where do you suppose he gets all of his things from?" Iscia asked quietly.

"Maybe he stole them," William whispered back.

Suddenly the cab jumped. William and Iscia flew up off the seat.

"Sorry," Phil yelled through the plexiglass that separated the driver's compartment from the passenger seats.

He turned the wheel to the side, and the cab swerved around some traffic on the road.

"Do you think he has a driver's license?" Iscia sounded worried.

"Doesn't seem like it," William replied.

"But isn't it kind of cool? Being picked up by an ancient android and taken on a trip around the world?" Iscia was smiling now.

William didn't respond. Benjamin had said that the orbulator code was difficult, and that it would kill anyone who tried but couldn't solve it completely. And the orbulator code had been difficult, but not that difficult. He had a feeling that the trials weren't over yet.

After a breathless trip through the streets of London, Phil finally pulled over and stopped at the curb. He turned off the engine and then swiveled around to face them, sliding open a little window in the plexiglass divider.

"It was nice to meet you, Iscia," he said with a smile. "Here's a little money. You can catch a train from over there. Anywhere you want to go." Phil pointed to a large train station a short distance away.

"Huh?" Iscia was afraid.

"Train?" William couldn't believe his own ears. "What are you talking about?"

"I can only bring the one who's solving the pyramid," Phil said. "And that's you, William. That means that she can't come. It's too dangerous."

William and Iscia exchanged looks.

"That's how I'm programmed," Phil said apologetically. "If I'm not remembering it completely wrong."

"You can't just drop me off here," Iscia protested, "in the middle of the night." Fear shone in her eyes.

"Sorry," Phil said with a shrug. "Those are the rules."

"Do you think this is okay?" Iscia said, fixing her eyes on William. "That I have to get out here?"

William shook his head. He was so shocked that he didn't know what to say.

"We're going to retrieve the orbulator," Phil explained. "It's in a rather risky location. Far riskier than this place."

"Risk schmisk." Iscia snorted dismissively. "I thought we were in this together."

"If you force her to get out here," William said, opening

the door on his side of the cab, "then I'm getting out too."

"But . . . ," Phil protested. "You're the only one who's solved the pyramid. You *have* to come with me."

"Not if I don't want to," William said firmly.

Phil looked at them. He didn't seem to quite know what to say. "You know that this is very dangerous?" He watched Iscia.

"Yes." She nodded.

"And you know that there's a chance you two will never come back?"

"Yes." She nodded again. "But I'm willing to take the chance."

"And you know that the pyramid is just the first code? And that the last one is much harder?"

"That we did not know!" William looked at the Orbulator Agent in shock.

"Oh." A look of concern came over Phil's face. "I suppose there are a few things I've forgotten to mention to you. I've become a little absentminded over the years."

He twisted the key in the ignition, turned the steering wheel, and sped away.

28

Phil stopped the car on a dark side street near a bridge.

"Here we are then," he said. "Let's get going."

William peered out the window. He could just make out the contours of the large Palace of Westminster and Big Ben, towering into the dark night sky.

Phil nodded to something outside the cab. "Also, we need to be careful."

William noticed a police car parked a little way down the street.

They got out of the cab and shut the door.

"In here," Phil whispered. He backed into a dark courtyard behind them.

William and Iscia did the same. From there, they peered warily out, their eyes watchful. One of the doors on the police car opened, and a policeman came into view. He yawned and stretched.

"There's only one," William said.

The policeman walked around his car a couple of times before he continued over to the end of the bridge and leaned forward, putting his elbows on the railing. He stood that way with his back to them, staring out at the Thames.

"Looks like he's bored," Iscia said.

"We have to get over there unnoticed." Phil pointed at the enormous clock tower on the other side of the street.

"Now."

The three of them darted across the wide street. It was the middle of the night, and there was almost no traffic. A car went by behind them. William and Iscia followed Phil along the railing, climbed over the fence, and kept going until they came to the back of the tower.

"Now what?" Iscia said.

"Hold on." Phil started searching through his pockets. "There you are," he said, and pulled out something that looked like a small metal door. He lifted the door up toward the stone wall on the clock tower. He was about to place the small door inside a squarish depression in the wall but stopped as the sound of squealing tires pierced the quiet night.

William turned and saw a black car stop out on the street. He recognized it as one of the Institute's cars that was capable of going extremely fast.

The driver's-side door opened, and a tall figure stepped out. It was Goffman. He stopped and peered around the dark street. Then he fixed his gaze on the huge clock tower. Cornelia's mechanical hand gleamed in the light from the streetlamps. Even from this distance, William could tell that Goffman's eyes looked completely crazy. His one eye was darting this way and that, just like Cornelia Strangler's eye had always done.

William felt Iscia stiffen beside him.

"William," Iscia whispered, "look." She pointed.

William followed her finger with his eyes and saw the policeman approaching Goffman.

"You can't park there!" the policeman yelled, gesturing at Goffman's car.

Goffman raised the mechanical hand. A thick beam shot out of it and bathed the street in blue light before it hit the policeman in the middle of his chest. He collapsed.

Goffman started walking across the street. A car had to slam on its brakes to avoid hitting him.

In only a few seconds, Goffman would see them.

"No time to lose," Phil said, and placed the metal slab into the rectangular depression in the stone.

The small metal door started clicking.

Faster and faster.

It began to grow. It doubled in size with every click and soon was the size of a normal door.

Phil grabbed the handle and pulled the door open.

"Get inside," he said, motioning at William and Iscia.

Phil jumped in after them and pulled the door shut behind him.

The last thing William saw before the door closed was Goffman racing toward them with his mechanical hand raised.

There came another series of clicking noises from the door. William stepped backward without taking his eyes off the door, which began to fold itself up. It got smaller and smaller until it turned into a small metal door again and flopped onto the floor.

Phil bent down and picked the door up. He stuck it back in one of his large pockets and turned to William.

There were distant pounding sounds from the other side of the wall. Goffman wanted to enter, but there was no longer any door to go through.

"Do you think he's going to get in?" Iscia whispered.

"It's going to take him a little while at any rate," Phil said. "We have to get going."

29

"Could you push that button over there," Phil said, and pointed at a square stone that protruded from the wall behind William.

William pushed the button, and it disappeared into the wall with a soft scraping sound.

Suddenly the floor shook violently. So violently that William had to hold on to the wall to keep from falling over. It rumbled beneath them.

Then the whole floor started moving downward. There was another scraping sound as the massive stone floor ground against the walls on its way down. William pulled back into the middle, and they steadied one another as the floor beneath them sank deeper and deeper.

"It's an elevator," William said. "A secret elevator inside

Big Ben." Even though he was scared, another part of him found this incredibly cool. Imagine that . . . a secret elevator inside one of the world's most famous landmarks.

"Pretty cool, huh?" Phil said with a smile. "I made it myself."

William looked up. They'd already traveled some distance.

And with a jerk and a deep, resounding boom, the floor stopped. William stood there, waiting, but nothing happened.

"Could you push that one," Phil said, pointing to a rusty metal bump sticking out of the wall beside Iscia.

Iscia raised her hand and pushed the button. The moment she did it, a rumbling could be heard from deep within the stone wall in front of them. The wall started slowly moving to the side, revealing profound darkness. A foul-smelling rush of air flowed toward them. The air down here felt like it was hundreds of years old, and the hairs on William's head stood up.

Phil hurried into the darkness beyond the door. He disappeared, and everything went eerily silent.

Then there was a faint click, and a dusty lightbulb in the ceiling flickered to life. It gave off just enough light for them to make out their surroundings. They were in a long tunnel.

Phil searched through his pockets.

"I just had it. It used to be right here," he said woefully.

He pulled a red phone booth the size of a matchbox out of one pocket and then stuffed it back again in annoyance and continued looking while muttering to himself.

Finally he found what he was looking for. "Here it is," he said with a satisfied smile. He leaned over and placed what he'd found on the floor. Then he straightened up again and took a couple of steps back.

"Cover your eyes," he instructed.

William put his hands over his eyes and waited. Right after that there was a loud zap and a series of clicks. Then it was quiet again.

"Okay," Phil said. "Come on."

When William opened his eyes, there was a golf cart right in front of them. Phil walked over to it and ran his hand over the hood.

"This will speed things up," he said, and motioned to William and Iscia. "Climb in." And with an elegant bow, Phil hopped in behind the wheel.

William and Iscia sat down in the backseat.

"Hold on tight," Phil said, stepping on the gas. "I'm going to have to drive fast."

The golf cart sped off across the crumbling floor just as there was an explosion from inside the elevator shaft they had come from.

"They blasted through the wall?" Iscia shouted.

"Probably did," Phil shouted back. "It will still take time to get down here. Hold tight."

30

William clung to a handle while he stared into the seemingly
endless tunnel ahead of them. Phil drove like a wild man.
Every time the cart almost careened into the wall, he gave a
quick laugh, as if he found this unbelievably fun.

"Who made these tunnels?" William called out.

"The same person who made Big Ben," Phil said, and
then paused for a moment for dramatic effect. "Me."

"You?" William gasped.

"You made Big Ben?" Iscia exclaimed.

"Yup. Well, not all by myself, of course. I designed it,
and some other people built it. Big Ben is a clever entrance
to the tunnels below. And the tunnels are an unbelievably
practical way to get around."

"Are there more secret entrances up there?" Iscia asked.

"Yes . . . many," Phil said slyly. "And all over the world. The Eiffel Tower . . . the pyramids . . . the Great Wall . . . I designed most of them."

Phil turned the wheel, and the golf cart veered around a corner. "Oops. I almost forgot that I have to stop somewhere and pick something up."

"What?" William asked.

"Patience, my young code breaker. Every dance begins with the first step," Phil said.

A few minutes later the golf cart abruptly stopped in front of an unstable rock wall at the end of the long tunnel.

Phil jumped out and walked over to a large metal door. After a bit of looking, he pulled a bunch of keys out of a pocket.

He had to try a number of keys before he found the right one. There was a click, and Phil pulled it open.

"Wait here," he said, taking a flashlight out of his pants pocket. "I'll be back in a jiffy." He vanished into the darkness beyond.

"I have to see what's in there," William said, getting out of the cart.

He proceeded over to the door and peered in. All he saw was Phil's flashlight sweeping through the darkness. He was doing some serious rummaging around in there. The beam of light hit something that looked like a large military tank.

"Do you see anything?" Iscia asked.

"I need to get a closer look," William said, walking into the darkness. "I think we've been here before."

An icy cold current of air hit him. It was the kind of cold draft that went right through the body and settled deeply into the marrow of one's bones. And now William was sure: He had been here before. Every nerve in his skin was taut.

This room was big . . . bigger than big.

It was gigantic.

He looked around and spotted a light switch on the wall next to the door. He walked over and turned it on. Electrical crackling sounds could be heard above him, and one by one the aging lights on the ceiling came on.

Soon the entire enormous hall was bathed in a sparkling yellow light.

Phil stopped what he was doing and looked over at William.

"Thanks," he said. "I'd forgotten there were lights in here."

William scanned the tanks and airships strewn over the massive, cavernous hall. It looked like a messy boy's bedroom, only everything was a thousand times bigger.

Images of what had happened the last time William was here flashed in front of his eyes. His grandfather finding the cryonic freezer, Abraham Talley almost killing him, the flood that had upended everything in the hall.

Phil continued in among all the military tanks and battleships.

"I have to come back another time and do a little tidying in here," he said, and started emptying things out of his pockets. He collected the items in a long row on the floor, and soon there was a host of little cars, planes, and boats in front of him.

"It's totally unbelievable how much accumulates when you don't empty your pockets thoroughly every once in a while."

"Is that why we came down here?" William asked. "So you could empty your pockets?"

"Yes," Phil said, pointing his remote at all the things on the floor. "Do you have any idea how heavy it is to walk around lugging all this with you?" He pressed a button on the remote, and one by one the cars, planes, and boats grew to their normal size.

"But we're also here to pick something up," Phil continued, looking around.

"What?" William asked.

"That, over there." Phil pointed to an enormous submarine. "I hope it's survived the careless treatment it's received in here. It was specially built to tolerate extreme depths."

William watched while Phil walked over to the submarine, shrank it, and stuffed it into a coat pocket.

"Well, we have to move on," Phil said, quickly walking back over to William. "Emma is waiting."

"Who's Emma?" William said, following Phil.

"No point trying to explain that now," Phil said. "Much better for you to see her with your own eyes."

31

The golf cart squealed around a corner and continued down a long corridor.

"There are many vast reservoirs down here," Phil said. "Most of them were built in the eighteenth century and hold enormous amounts of water."

"Really?" William said, glancing nervously at Iscia.

"We have to go down to one specific reservoir," Phil said. "That's where Emma is. She'll take us where we're going."

After a few minutes of wild-man driving, the golf cart stopped in front of yet another huge, rusty iron door. In the middle of the door was an old brass sign that said DANGER: DEEP WATER.

Phil hopped out of the golf cart and went up to the

door. William and Iscia followed. William cast one quick glance over his shoulder. He didn't see any signs of anyone following them. Yet.

Phil grabbed the large, vaguely nautical-looking handle on the door and pulled it toward himself. They heard the creak of old, rusty metal.

"This reservoir was built over a natural water source, so it's impossible to drain it. No one knows how deep it is. A perfect place for Emma. Come on." Phil proceeded through the doorway and waved for William and Iscia to follow.

Once they were all inside, Phil closed the door.

William looked around. They were standing on a sort of pier, which sloped down into the dark water. Large columns ran from the ceiling into the water.

"This is part of London's old water supply," Phil explained. "It's nearly two hundred years old, from the Victorian era, to be completely precise." Phil checked his watch. "Well, that's enough of a history lesson. We don't have much time."

He pulled a small, round bathysphere no bigger than a rubber duck out of his pocket and carefully placed it in the water. As he let go of it, it stayed put, bobbing on the surface.

"Back up," Phil said, and pointed his remote. A few seconds later the bathysphere in front of them was full-size.

William jumped because there was a sudden boom on the iron door behind them.

"They found us already?" Phil called out. "Irritating."

The door boomed again.

"He's coming in," Iscia yelled.

"Wait a little," Phil said, and started rooting through his pockets. He pulled out a little red double-decker London bus. "Good thing I didn't leave everything back in the bunker."

He hurried over to the iron door and set the London bus down in front of it. After taking several steps back, he pointed the remote control at the bus and pushed the button.

The little bus started shaking before it grew at a shocking rate. William and Iscia backed up until the edge of the water made them stop.

A full-size London bus stood before them now.

"That ought to hold him a little longer," Phil said, and hurried over to the bathysphere. In a couple of bounds, he jumped onto its roof, bent down, and grabbed a round locking wheel. He turned the wheel and opened a hatch down into the bathysphere.

"In you go!" he called out.

William hurried over onto the bell and climbed through the round hatch. Iscia was right behind him. William turned and waited for Phil to climb in as well. But he was still standing on the outside.

"Aren't you coming?" William asked.

"I have to stay here and keep him from getting in," Phil responded. "You guys will figure it out. I'll be along as soon as I can."

William surveyed the inside of the bathysphere. There were two seats and a control panel. Large glass windows provided a view into the dark water.

"But we don't know where we're going," William called back.

"Down!" Phil exclaimed. "Everything you need to know is in the manual." He pointed to a book on a small table next to where William had just set the orbulator.

"And Emma . . . ?" William began, but was cut short by a substantial explosion out in the hall.

"Get out of here," Phil yelled. "I don't have time to explain. You'll recognize Emma right away when you see her. She'll take you to the Mariana Trench."

Another powerful explosion shook the bathysphere, and Phil slammed the hatch closed over them.

32

William and Iscia sat for a moment, listening to the noises outside the bathysphere.

"Do you think Goffman made it through the door?" Iscia asked. She looked worried. "We shouldn't leave Phil behind like this."

"We have no choice," William said. He picked up the manual from the little table. The cover said BATHYSPHERE MANUAL FOR TELEPORTATION in all caps. Underneath the title there was a picture of a bathysphere, like the one they were sitting in.

"Teleportation?" William mumbled. He opened the manual and started reading.

Two minutes later they were on their way down.

William sat at the controls, piloting the bathysphere into

the abyss. After skimming through the manual, William had picked up the most important points: Push the handle forward to dive and pull it back to rise. Pretty simple, actually. The manual said they had to go down to a depth of fifteen hundred feet.

William glanced at the depth gauge on the control panel, which already registered a depth of more than three hundred feet.

"Who could Emma be?" Iscia mused, peering into the darkness outside.

In all the commotion, William had completely forgotten Emma.

"I have a feeling we'll find out soon," he said, pushing the handle even farther forward.

They continued their descent into the void. Everything was totally dark around them. The only indication that they were moving was the depth gauge. Soon it showed that they were at a depth of almost twelve hundred feet. There was still no sign they were going to reach the bottom.

"There's something out there," Iscia said excitedly, pointing out the window.

William looked in the direction she was pointing.

"I don't see . . . ," he began, but stopped when he noticed something glowing in the dark water.

At first it was just a dim light. Like a solitary little light-bulb floating in the water. Then the light grew clearer and larger. And as the light came closer, William noticed more lights, a string of them. It looked like there were hundreds of them, in all the colors of the rainbow. It was as if they were dancing in the darkness below them. The lights came closer and closer, until they covered the entire window.

"What is that?" he whispered.

He was staring at the undulating lights. There was something hypnotic about the way they moved. William felt his body going numb. He glanced at the depth gauge. It said they were more than fifteen hundred feet down. He didn't know if it was the dancing lights or the pressure or both that was doing it, but he suddenly felt weak. And his head was tingling, as if he were about to faint.

"Do you feel that too?" he said, without taking his eyes off the lights.

"The tingling?" Iscia said. William could hear from her voice that she was also having trouble.

"Yes," William said.

"You think it might have something to do with that?" she said, pointing at the control panel in front of them.

William forced himself to look away from the hypnotic lights outside.

There was a clocklike meter on the control panel that said OXYGEN on it. The arrow was approaching the red zone.

William suddenly realized what was making them so

sluggish. "We're running out of . . . air," he said. His lungs hurt as he spoke.

"What do we do?" Iscia wheezed back. She sounded like she had asthma.

William couldn't give up now. He had to fight. His eyes moved back to the control panel. They stopped at a switch that said SPOTLIGHTS.

William reached out and put his index finger on the switch. It was difficult to move, as if he were suspended in gelatin. And he was breathing like he'd just sprinted a fifty-yard race.

He pushed the button.

A hum started somewhere above them. And a powerful beam of light shot out into the darkness. If William had had more air in his lungs, he would have screamed at the sight facing him. Instead, he emitted only a weak gasp.

A colossal octopus was floating in the darkness outside the bathysphere. Its body was the size of a whole house. And the eight tentacles had to be as long as soccer fields.

But this was no normal octopus. It was covered in lights, all over its tentacles and its body. And only now did William realize that its body was made of some kind of metal.

"It's an enormous robotic octopus," William wheezed, his lungs burning from lack of air.

Iscia didn't respond. William looked at the oxygen meter. The needle was almost completely at the bottom.

"Iscia?" William said. She still had her eyes open, but her breathing was labored.

William turned around, grabbed the control stick, and pulled it toward him.

"I'm going to get you up to the surface."

William wasn't willing to sacrifice Iscia, not for anything, not even for antiluridium.

Suddenly something banged into them. One of the massive tentacles coiled around the bathysphere and held them back. And in the collision, the glass in front of William had cracked. A thin stream of water poured in.

William looked around the bathysphere in desperation. The immense tentacles outside squeezed harder, and he heard the glass beginning to give way.

Then he noticed it.

He leaned forward and studied the tentacle through the glass. Small electronic lights blinked at him, but that wasn't what had caught William's attention. It was a little metal plate attached to the end of the tentacle that said MODEL: EMMA 2000.

"Emma?" William said out loud to himself. "Are you Emma?"

"Did Phil send us down here just to get killed by a mechanical octopus?" Iscia suddenly gasped.

William jumped. "Welcome back." He smiled wanly. "I'm trying to figure out what Emma here wants."

He glanced down at the manual he was holding and opened it to the index. He ran his finger down the list until he came to the words he was looking for, the ones that began with the letter *E*.

Turning to the page he wanted, he said, "Listen!" Every word he said hurt, and it was hard to focus on the text in front of him. But he couldn't give up now. They had to do this.

"Establish communication with teleported electro-octopi using radio waves. . . ."

After struggling his way through the rest of the instructions, William took the bathysphere's radio in his hand. The speaker on the wall crackled. He turned a knob and tuned the radio to the correct wavelength. Suddenly the crackling went away, and pleasant elevator music poured out of the speaker.

William and Iscia exchanged looks.

"Is that a radio channel?" she gasped, her face pale. "Fast. There's almost no air left."

William checked the manual again. This was the right channel. William didn't know what to expect, but this couldn't be right. He was about to try tuning it some more when the music stopped, and a pleasant female voice came through the speaker.

"Welcome to Emma 2000," it said. "The best way to travel. All you need to do is plot the coordinates for your destination, and Emma 2000 will take you the rest of the way."

"Do you know the coordinates for the Mariana Trench?" William wheezed, looking at Iscia.

"No," she said. "But I bet that does." She leaned forward and tapped on a world atlas hanging on the wall. It said OCEANS OF THE WORLD in big blue letters on the cover.

"Can you find it?" William gasped, and glanced down at the oxygen level. The needle had hit red now.

Iscia hunted feverishly though the pages.

"We don't have much time!" William coughed.

"Here it is," she said. "Let's see. Eleven degrees twenty-one minutes north." She paused, breathing rapidly. "And one hundred forty-two degrees twelve minutes east."

William entered the coordinates.

It was quiet for a moment. He felt the last remaining air leave his body. It hadn't worked. Iscia slumped beside him. Then he heard the woman's voice again: "Destination: the Pacific Ocean. Fasten your seat belts. We will teleport in ten, nine, eight, seven . . ."

William listened to the countdown. Iscia had collapsed again.

"Three, two, one . . ."

ZAP!

33

The bathysphere landed in the water with a tremendous splash.

William leaned over Iscia. He opened a porthole in the ceiling, and fresh air poured in. Iscia stirred. She took a deep breath and opened her eyes. "That was close," William said.

Iscia shuddered and sat up. The bathysphere bobbed up and down a few times before it settled.

"Look over there," Iscia cried, pointing out the window.

One of the mechanical tentacles slid off the top of the bell and down into the water. Through the thick glass, they could see the silhouette of the massive octopus as it continued down into the depths and disappeared with a flash of light.

"Do you think it's teleporting back where we came from?" Iscia asked.

"Sure," William said. "That must be where its base is."

William and Iscia looked at each other for a long moment, and William knew they were thinking the same thing.

How were they going to go down into the trench in this little bathysphere? Phil had said they had to go all the way to the bottom. They were going to need a submarine for that, the one Phil had picked up down in the bunker.

William looked at the crack in the glass in front of him. The floor of the bathysphere was covered with water. He knew that even if they replaced the glass, the bathysphere had taken a beating and might not be able to handle the pressure down there. They could be crushed long before they reached the bottom.

"What do we do now?" Iscia asked, peering out the window.

Half of the bathysphere was underwater. A school of playful dolphins swam by in the bright blue water right in front of them.

William didn't answer, not because he didn't want to, but because he didn't know what to say. He didn't know how they could get down to the bottom, at least not with the equipment they had available.

"Well, we can't just sit around up here moping," William finally said. He stood up and opened the roof hatch. Salty marine air flooded in.

Not long after that, William and Iscia were sitting on the

roof of the bathysphere. The waves lapped against the sides. If it weren't for the stressful situation they found themselves in, it would have been an idyllic moment, something out of a travel brochure: the bright blue water, the sky, the warm sunshine.

"Is that land over there?" Iscia asked, pointing to the horizon.

"Don't think so," William replied.

Iscia's gaze followed a school of fish.

They heard a tremendous splash behind them, and a large wave hit William, washing him right off the bathysphere and into the sea. He swallowed mouthfuls of water as he flailed his arms to get back to the surface. Finally William broke through the surface and gasped for air.

"William!" Iscia yelled.

He looked in the direction her voice had come from. She was clinging to the bathysphere. Something big and black was obscuring the sun.

It was an enormous submarine.

A hatch on the top of the submarine opened, and a figure popped out.

The figure raised its arm and waved. "Are you guys ready?"

34

"How did it go?" was the first thing William said after Phil had locked the submarine's hatch.

William noticed a big gash on the back of Phil's head. The android's white puzzle-piece skin had been torn away, and the workings underneath were visible.

"Are you hurt?" Iscia said.

"Hm?" Phil said, looking over at her.

Iscia pointed to the gash on the back of his head. Phil felt around with his hand.

"Oh, it heals fast," he said, flapping his hand a bit as if this were the most trivial thing in the world. "You should have seen me after the meteorite that did away with the dinosaurs."

"So, how did it go?" William asked again.

"How did what go?" Phil replied, turning to face William.

"How did it go when you stayed behind in London just now?"

Phil stared blankly at William for a moment as if he had no idea what William was talking about. Then his eyes lit up.

"Oh . . . that. Yes, that went quite well," he said, then pointed to a round hole in the floor in front of them.

"We have to get down there." Phil climbed down the ladder that stuck up from the hole. He gestured for William and Iscia to follow him.

They entered the submarine's control room. The walls around them were covered with knobs, meters, wires, and pipes. There was beeping and whirring and ticking.

Phil raised the periscope and looked through it. "Push that button," he instructed, waving his hand at Iscia. "And, William, you'll need to pull down the control lever when I give the word."

He pointed to a lever sticking out of the wall.

They followed Phil's instructions, and the enormous submarine started to descend. It shuddered, creaked, and bubbled around them as thousands of tons of steel sank down into the dark depths.

"Are you sure that isn't a problem?" Iscia asked, pointing at the gash on the back of Phil's head.

Phil raised his hand and felt around. "Oops," he said,

and looked a little concerned. "I had totally forgotten about that." He rolled up one jacket sleeve and pushed some buttons on a little control panel on his forearm.

Seconds later, the white skin dangling from his head wound began to fold its way upward, contracting. The gash grew smaller and smaller until the wound was gone.

"There," Phil said with a smile. "All better." He turned to the wall and started pulling levers and pushing buttons while muttering to himself. He turned on a screen that was mounted on the wall.

"They didn't have screens back when this submarine was built, did they?" William asked.

"That's right," Phil said. "I had to install this one myself. It makes the job much easier."

Phil leaned to the side and pushed a button on the wall, and pleasant jazz music filled the space from a small speaker beside the screen.

"You guys can relax for a bit now," Phil said. "It's a long way down." He turned and left through a small iron door.

William sat down on the floor and leaned his back against the wall. Iscia sat down beside him.

They sat like this in silence for a while, listening to all the strange sounds that surrounded them. The beeping and ticking from the instruments. Menacing creaking sounds from the hull and the water that rushed past as the huge metal sub descended into the deep.

After some time had passed, William looked up at the depth meter. They were already halfway down to the bottom of the trench. The submarine dived quickly, and William's ears and head had started to hurt. He could feel every heartbeat like a sledgehammer inside his head.

"Do you realize how deep we are right now?" Iscia asked, without looking at him. "These submarines aren't built for depths like these."

"But Phil says he modified this one and that it'll be totally fine," William said, trying to reassure himself as much as Iscia.

He got up and walked over to the TV screen on the wall. It showed only black. William tapped on it a couple of times. "Is this broken?"

"No," Iscia replied. "It's been like this for a while, totally dark. The sunlight doesn't penetrate this far down."

William looked at the depth gauge. The needle showed that they were almost twenty thousand feet below the surface.

"Look at that!" William pointed to the screen. A glowing fish with pointy spikes and an enormous mouth full of razor-sharp teeth swam by.

Phil walked into the control room. "Get ready," he said. "We're almost there."

"Almost where?" William peered at the screen. "There's nothing out there!" The fish was gone, and once again the screen showed only black.

"You'll see soon," Phil responded. "I haven't been here for a while. It's a little weird to be back with someone who's solved the pyramid."

"How long has it been since you were last here?" Iscia asked.

"Oh," Phil said, calculating. "A few million years. Give or take." William and Iscia exchanged glances.

"There it is!" Phil exclaimed, pointing to the monitor.

"I see it," Iscia said, stepping closer. She was staring at a small gray spot that was growing on the screen.

"It looks like a pyramid," she said.

"That's right." Phil's voice quivered with anticipation.

"Why is there a pyramid down here at the bottom of the Mariana Trench?" Iscia turned to Phil.

"Because this is a perfect place for a pyramid," he responded. "Especially if you don't want anyone to find it."

"But why a pyramid?" Iscia asked with a determined voice.

"Have you ever been in the Sahara?" Phil asked.

"No!" Iscia said.

"It's sort of the same shape as the great pyramids you find there," Phil said. "Egypt for example. Only, the pyramid shape is also a perfect structure if you want something to withstand great pressure, like we find down here."

"It looks small," William said. He was staring at the pyramid, utterly transfixed, unable to take his eyes off it.

"Oh, it's much bigger than the ones in Egypt," Phil muttered. He was fiddling with some buttons on the wall. "Three times bigger, actually."

"Three times?" William repeated, alarmed. "Is this one made of stone too?"

"Metal," Phil said. "Like that." He nodded at the orbulator, which was lying on the floor. "They're actually accurate copies of each other."

William looked at the orbulator. It was glowing now, although not just the symbols. It was as if the metal itself was beginning to glow. It was pulsing, and with each beat it grew brighter.

"Why is it glowing?" William asked.

"We're establishing contact," Phil said.

"With who?"

"With that, there." Phil pointed. The pyramid on the monitor was glowing now too.

The light from it was pulsing in time with the orbulator.

"You'd better grab on to something," Phil said. "This is usually where things get a little rough."

A beam of light shot out from the pyramid on the ocean floor. The beam pierced the dark waters with lightning speed and hit the sub, making the whole structure shake violently. William fell backward and hit the floor.

Then everything exploded in white light.

35

William opened his eyes and scanned the surroundings. They were still inside the sub. Iscia sat next to him on the floor rubbing her shoulder.

"That hurt," she moaned. "It's like we crashed."

"This way," Phil said, and motioned for them to follow him. "Sometimes tractor beams can be a bit rough."

"Tractor beams?" William said, stumbling to his feet.

William and Iscia scrambled after Phil out the door.

Phil began opening the hatch in the ceiling.

"What are you doing?" Iscia protested. "There's tons of water out there."

"Not anymore," Phil said, and pushed open the hatch. Bright light shot in through the round opening. "Come!" Phil climbed out the hatch and disappeared in the whiteness.

William was about to climb after him when he felt Iscia's hand on his arm.

"William," she said. "We don't know if it's safe."

"We've come too far to stop now," he replied, and climbed through.

William stood on top of the submarine, which seemed to be stranded in a huge white room.

"Come down here," Phil shouted, waving at him from below. He was standing next to the sub.

"What is this?" Iscia said. She climbed to her feet and stopped next to William.

"I have no idea," William said. "Let's find out!"

A minute later William and Iscia stood next to Phil. Except for the huge submarine, which lay dry-docked in the middle of the white room, there was nothing here. Only white.

"Where are we?" Iscia looked every bit as scared as William felt.

"Welcome," a female voice said. The voice seemed to be coming from all around them.

"Thanks," Phil said. "It's good to be back."

"It's been two million, eight hundred, and fifty-four years, two hundred and seventy-four days, two hours, and fifty-four minutes since you were last here," the voice said.

"Whoa, time sure does fly!" Phil said, smiling; he seemed surprised.

William leaned over to him and whispered, "Who are we talking to, actually?"

"Me." The voice came from somewhere behind them now.

William turned around and saw a woman with long dark hair wearing a white robe. She looked like an angel and was so dazzlingly beautiful that William could neither look at her nor away from her. She smiled as her eyes landed first on Iscia, then on William, and finally on Phil.

"You look tired, Philip," she said, her voice filled with concern. "You need to rest soon."

"Thanks." Phil looked down as if the word "rest" embarrassed him.

"What is she?" Iscia whispered.

"I'm a representation of the data stored down here," the woman replied.

"Like a hologram?" William asked.

"Precisely," the woman said, and smiled. She paused and looked at them with bright blue eyes.

"Who solved the pyramid?" she asked.

"*He* did." Phil pointed at William.

The woman's eyes moved to William. And he suddenly felt the urge to hide. What had he gotten himself and Iscia into?

"And what's *your* name?" the woman said, and moved closer.

"William Wenton," William said, paying close attention to her face as he said his name. There was no reaction, except for that pleasant smile.

"Hello, William Wenton," the woman said, and stopped in front of him. "Perhaps you are wondering who I am?"

William gulped. His mouth was totally dry. So he merely nodded.

"I am the last representation of the civilization that lived down here," she said, still with a smile on her lips.

"We both are actually," Phil corrected her, giving his own smile.

"That's right," she said, and looked at him. "We are actually two . . . the only two beings left from the vast civilization that once flourished here. Where you saw the pyramid, we used to live in a great underwater city, all built from metal—but only the pyramid has survived the eons of pressure. We call it the Lost City."

William was taken aback. "A computer program?" he said.

"I can take many forms," the woman continued. "And through me, you have access to all the knowledge the civilization down here amassed through many millions of years of research."

"That's a lot of information." Phil sounded proud.

"And you can access all that information if you pass the final test." The angelic figure looked directly at William now.

"As you surely know," she continued, "a great deal depends on you."

William nodded meekly. He suddenly felt very small. The thought of being responsible for all the knowledge that this civilization had gathered over millions of years was daunting.

"What happened to those who lived here?" Iscia asked.

"Many millions of years ago, humankind was forced to leave the earth through the Crypto Portal," the woman said in a calm voice. "A small group of people escaped when the luridium took over the bodies of those on the surface. They fled down here. Into the deep. Here, they were safe."

She paused for a moment before continuing, to let that information sink in.

"They lived down here for thousands of generations. Millions of years. With their eyes on a single goal the entire time: to find a way to defeat the luridium if it should ever return to earth." The woman paused and looked at William with calm blue eyes.

"And did they?" William asked. "Did they find a way?"

"Yes, they did," the woman said, and smiled. "After countless generations of trying and failing, they finally came up with something that could defeat that seemingly unbeatable luridium."

"And what was it?" William gasped.

The woman looked at Phil again. "Do you have it with you?" she asked.

Phil nodded and stuck his hand in one of his large pockets. He pulled out a small pyramid and placed it on the floor in front of them. William recognized it as the orbulator.

"There it is," the woman said softly.

Phil pointed his remote toward the pyramid.

"You'd better step back," he said, and motioned for William and Iscia to move.

They did as they were told.

And with a zap and a bright flash of light, the pyramid grew until it towered over them.

"This is the orbulator," the woman said. "This is the result of millions of years of experimentation. And it will soon belong to you . . . if you pass the final test."

"But," William started. He felt dizzy and had a tremendous headache. "What is it?"

"It's the most powerful weapon in the world," the woman said. "The only thing that can defeat the luridium."

She paused. Just stood there, regarding William with her bright eyes. And that's when William noticed. He hadn't seen it before, because of the white background. But now, when she was standing in front of the metal pyramid, he could see that she was transparent. Only slightly. But it frightened him.

"And?" Iscia said impatiently. "What is it that can defeat luridium?"

"If William passes the final test," the woman said softly, "I will tell you."

"What happens if I don't pass?" William asked, his voice trembling from fear.

"Then you will have to stay down here," the woman replied. "Both of you."

"For how long?" William was afraid he already knew the answer.

"The rest of your lives. And Philip will travel back and continue his search for someone else who can solve the orbulator."

"And if William passes the test?" Iscia said.

"Then the orbulator is yours, and you can return to the surface. All of the information will then be stored on it, and you can use it to fight the luridium."

And with those words, she was gone.

36

William looked around. Everything was so dazzling white that it was hard to see where the floor ended and the walls began.

"I don't like this at all," Iscia said.

William didn't like it either, but he didn't say that out loud. He needed to remain calm.

"Phil's gone too," he said. "And the sub. How did everything disappear like that?"

"Because now everything is up to us . . . ," Iscia said. "Or you, to be more exact."

"The code probably has something to do with this." William pointed at the pyramid.

"It's too big to manipulate," Iscia said. She walked over to it and placed her hand on the surface. "It must weigh thousands of tons now."

William looked up at the huge pyramid. It was strange to think that he had been carrying this thing around with him.

"Well," he said, and braced himself. "I can't just stand around like this all day. I have to do something."

He took off his jacket and threw it on the ground. Rolled up his sleeves and looked at the surface in front of him. The pyramid wall filled his whole range of view. He closed his eyes and waited. If there was a code here, his vibrations surely would let him know.

But nothing happened.

"The luridium inside of you can't help you here," the woman's pleasant voice said.

William opened his eyes and looked around. The woman was nowhere to be seen. He looked over at Iscia, who was standing right behind him.

"Did you hear that?" he asked.

"Hear what?" she said.

"Never mind." William returned his attention to the pyramid.

It *had* to be the code. Why else would it be here? Besides, there was nothing else here.

He focused all his attention on the strange symbols on the surface. If it was true that the luridium inside his own body didn't work down here, he would have to rely on his own inherent skills to solve this problem. And that was terrifying.

As William stood like that and let his thoughts race through his head, he suddenly noticed something on the surface of the pyramid. It was directly in front of him and had probably been there all along. But it was partly hidden among all the carved symbols.

It looked like a door.

William lifted his hand and touched the surface. The door was a square indentation. And very well hidden. There was no handle or lock.

"Do you see something?" William heard Iscia say. Her voice was distant, like she had moved farther away from him. But he knew that she was still right behind him.

William didn't answer. He focused all his attention on the door. Was he supposed to open it? How?

And now he saw that the door was divided into smaller pieces. Like a puzzle. A puzzle William had seen before. On Phil's skin. William had always had an exceptional visual memory. It was photographic. Something that came in good use when he solved codes.

William closed his eyes and pictured Phil with his mind's eye. He tried to reproduce every single detail. His head, arms, legs, and long coat. He mentally zoomed in on his face, remembering the white skin that seemed to be made up of small puzzle pieces. When William had first noticed Phil's skin, he had thought that it was some kind of gimmick. Like a cool look. A design.

Now he knew that there had to be more to it.

Maybe even a solution, or a clue, to the code that William now stood before.

While holding the mental image of Phil, William reached out and touched the door. He let his hand slide across the surface. All the little metal pieces were loose and could be moved around to make a different pattern. William started rearranging them to reproduce the same pattern he had seen on Phil's skin.

He used both hands to work. Moved the pieces around, faster and faster. It was as if he was in a trance, like when the luridium in his body helped him solve codes. Only now *he* was doing it. And not the luridium. It was a powerful feeling, and his belief in himself grew with each piece he moved into place.

Suddenly there was a deep rumble inside the door. William took a step back and watched as the heavy iron door slowly swung open.

"You did it," Iscia said from behind him.

"Not yet," William whispered. "I don't think it's over yet."

He stared into the darkness on the other side of the door. He knew he had to go in there. His heart beat heavily in his chest. He could feel the hairs on his head and his neck stand. And a shiver ran through his body as he took a step closer to the door.

"I'll come with you," he heard Iscia say.

"No," William said firmly. "You have to stay here, in case something happens."

He stopped right outside the door and looked in. There was nothing but darkness. If he was to solve the code completely, he knew he had to enter. Alone. Both his and Iscia's lives depended on it. And possibly the whole world. If he failed, they would be trapped down here forever.

William clenched his fists, and his whole body tensed as he walked into the darkness inside the pyramid.

37

William stopped in the darkness.

The inside of the pyramid was chilly. He could feel the cold against his face. And from the light that shone in through the door behind him, he could see how his breath turned into frost.

It was strange how dark it was in here. The light that came through the door should be enough to illuminate the surroundings. But it didn't.

Maybe there was nothing here. Maybe William had been mistaken in thinking that the solution to the code challenge was inside the pyramid.

"William?" Iscia called from outside.

"I'm fine," William replied. "There's nothing here."

"Then come out again," she said. "I have a bad—"

Iscia's voice was abruptly cut off as the door slammed shut behind William. He turned and headed for it but met only darkness. He slammed into the metal wall and came to a violent halt.

His hands desperately searched for the door. But the surface felt almost perfectly flat. Like polished metal. The door was gone.

And William was trapped.

The only things he could hear were the rapid in-and-out puffs of his breath. His heart beat hard and made his head hurt. And it felt even chillier now. Was it getting colder?

William beat the wall with his fists and shouted as loud as he could.

"ISCIA?"

His voice echoed in the darkness. He put his head against the surface. Listened. But there was no reply. Was Iscia still out there? Or had something happened to her? Was this all a trap?

"She can't hear you, William," a raspy voice said from the darkness behind him.

William froze. He immediately knew who it was.

"Turn around, William," the crackling voice continued.

Slowly William turned and looked into the darkness where the voice had come from.

"Good boy," the voice said. It was closer now. William could feel someone's rancid, cold breath on his face. But he still couldn't see anything except darkness.

"You've come a very long way to see me," the voice continued.

William kept quiet. He pushed himself against the wall behind him in a desperate effort to get away from the creature in the dark.

"What do you want?" William asked. His voice trembled with fear. All the memories about what had happened in the bunker under Victoria Station came back to him. He could feel Abraham Talley's dry, bony hands around his throat. He had been after the luridium in his body then—was that what he wanted now, too?

But how could he be here? He had disappeared through the Crypto Portal. Had he teleported down here? To the Mariana Trench? It seemed a little too extravagant. Going all the way to the Himalayas, just to teleport to the bottom of the ocean.

But Abraham Talley was here. William was sure of that. What did he want?

"What do you want?" William said again into the pitch black in front of him.

"Isn't that obvious?" Abraham hissed from the dark. "I want you, William. You belong with me. Together we could do great things."

"You are not here," William said. "You can't be. You're just a voice in my head. Go away!"

William pressed himself toward the cold wall at his back as lights started to blink around him. Thousands of tiny dots of light flickered to life. It was like a clear night sky filled with stars. Had William not been in the extreme situation that he was, he would probably have thought that this was one of the most beautiful things he had ever seen. But he had no time to think about beauty now, because together with the light, there also appeared something else. A dark figure stood before him. Partly illuminated by the tiny dots of light.

It was Abraham Talley.

He seemed younger now than the last time William had seen him. His shoulders were broad and powerful. His arms and hands sinewy and muscular. He was wearing a black suit, like he was on his way to a funeral. His beard was no longer gray, but black like the darkness that had just surrounded them. His dark eyes seemed to glitter from the light. And a smile spread across his face.

"Still don't think I'm here?" Abraham asked with his dry voice.

William didn't reply. He felt his whole life flashing before him. His childhood in England. The escape to Norway. His time at the Institute.

Was he about to die at Abraham's hands? Was this it? Was this how it all ended?

Desperately William looked around. There was nowhere for him to go. No escape. Nowhere to hide. Abraham Talley finally had him. And now he would finish what he had started in that bunker below London.

"I can give you anything you want, William," Abraham said.

"Then let me out of here," William said. "I want out."

Abraham let out a little chuckle.

"Nice try," he said. "I want you to join me," Abraham continued. "If you listen to your heart, you know that I'm right. Me and you . . . we're the same. We have the same fantastic stuff inside of us. Luridium. You know what I'm talking about. And I know you can feel the connection." Abraham came a step closer.

William pushed so hard against the wall behind him, his whole body hurt.

Abraham stopped right in front of him. He lifted a hand and placed it on William's shoulder.

"You can help me bring luridium back to earth," he said softly. "Back to where it belongs. Back for a new beginning and a new world."

"And what would happen to all the people on earth if the luridium returned?" William asked. He could feel anger rising in him.

"They would all be saved, of course," Abraham said.

"Saved?" William repeated.

"Yes," Abraham said, and smiled darkly. "They would merge with luridium, just like you and me. Only on a much greater scale."

"You're crazy," William said.

Abraham halted. His smile dropped away, and his dark eyes settled on William.

"What did you say?" he snarled.

Suddenly William didn't feel so brave anymore. Abraham leaned in even closer, and William almost choked on his acrid breath.

"You will give me the key to the box," Abraham said. "You will hand over the antiluridium. It belongs with me."

And now William understood what Abraham was trying to do. He was after the only thing humankind could use to prevent luridium from taking over the world. He wanted the antiluridium. All this was a clever ploy to trick William into giving it to him.

"NEVER!" William screamed at the top of his lungs. "I would rather die than give it to you!"

Abraham leaned back and looked at William. His face was almost startled. His eyes filled with surprise.

"You really mean that, don't you?" he said.

"Of course," William said, and pushed away from the wall.

"Then you're free to go," Abraham said. But now his voice seemed softer. Almost like a woman's voice.

"Excuse me?" William said.

There was a soft click behind William as the door opened. William turned and looked at it. White light from outside shone into the pyramid.

William turned to look at Abraham again, but he was gone.

William stepped outside the pyramid.

"William," Iscia said, and threw herself around his neck. "I thought it was a trap when the door slammed shut behind you."

"You're a tough negotiator," Phil said. He was standing a little farther away, together with the woman in white.

Iscia let go of William and looked at him.

"You made it, William," she said, her eyes welling up. "You made it out. You passed the test."

William looked at Phil.

"But Abraham . . ." William motioned behind him. "He was inside."

"It was a hologram, just like me," the woman said, and smiled softly. "We can't risk giving the antiluridium to someone who would buckle under pressure. Even if they are the best code breaker in the world."

Phil came toward William and stopped right in front of him. He extended his hand, and they shook.

"It's been a real pleasure getting to know you, William," he said. "It's time for you and Iscia to head back."

"You're not coming?" William said.

"My job is finally done," Phil said. "It's time for some recreation." He smiled. Then he pulled the remote from his pocket. He pointed it at the huge pyramid, and with a zap, it shrank back down.

"It's yours now, William," the woman said. "Use it with care."

Phil picked up the pyramid and handed it to William.

"Guard it with your life."

William nodded and took the small object in his hands.

38

William and Iscia were back in the submarine. It was cold
and dark. The deep thrum of the engine throbbed in the
distance. William looked around. He was alone in the
control room.

"Iscia?" he said, but there was no answer.

"Iscia!" he tried again, a little louder. All he could hear
was the hum of the submarine's engine.

The TV screen on the wall was dark. A couple of glowing fish swam by. There was no sign of the pyramid on the
seabed.

The orbulator sat on the floor in front of him. The mysterious symbols were pulsing. William could hardly fathom
that he was so close to an orbulator full of antiluridium.
But he had to wait to examine it. He had to find Iscia first.

"Iscia!" he yelled again.

"Here!" he suddenly heard from behind him.

William turned around and spotted her as she came through a small door at the far end of the room.

"Are we the only ones here?" She looked around.

"Yes," William replied. "Where were you?"

"I wound up down in the machine room," she said, trying to brush an oil stain off her jacket. She looked at the glowing orbulator on the floor. "What happened? Do you think we were inside that or inside the big pyramid down on the bottom?"

"I don't know," William replied. "But it looks like I succeeded in solving the code."

Iscia smiled. "Yes, you did." Her smile vanished as she continued. "I hope we see him again."

"Me too," William said. "But I do think Phil was ready for a break. Millions of years is a really long time. Just think: He was alive when the dinosaurs were."

Iscia nodded.

William walked over to one of the walls, which was covered with control instruments.

"There should be some kind of transmitter here somewhere," he said, his eyes sweeping over the blinking buttons.

"That?" Iscia pointed to an old radio.

William turned it on. The speaker crackled. When he

tuned it to the Emma 2000 wavelength, the crackling was replaced with pleasant elevator music.

"Welcome to Emma 2000," a familiar woman's voice said. "The best way to travel. All you need to do is plot the coordinates for your destination, and Emma 2000 will take you the rest of the way."

"Do you know the coordinates for London?" William looked at Iscia.

"To return, enter the return code: zero zero zero," the woman's voice said.

William exhaled and keyed in the code.

"Thank you," the voice said. "Localizing Emma 2000."

William took a couple of steps back and grabbed on to a handle on the wall. They stared at the dark screen.

"Can you believe Emma can dive this deep?" Iscia asked.

Before William had a chance to respond, something popped up in the darkness on the screen: a small glowing fleck, which was growing. Gradually, as it approached, William was able to make out the tentacles of the enormous teleportation octopus.

"Prepare to dock," the woman's voice announced.

A resounding boom echoed through the large submarine, and everything around them shook before it grew quiet again.

"Docking complete," the woman's voice announced. "Prepare to teleport."

William and Iscia stared at each other. A distant rumble spread through the metal hull.

"Teleporting in five . . . four . . . three . . . ," the voice said.

The electronics sparked. Iscia's hair stood on end.

"Two . . . one . . ."

ZAP!

It felt like they were being pulled upward with tremendous force before they flopped to the floor again. Powerful waves hit the outside of the submarine.

William and Iscia lay still, side by side. The submarine rocked back and forth like an enormous cradle.

It soon calmed down and then was completely still again.

"Do you think we're there?" Iscia asked, standing up.

"We're about to find out." William got to his feet. He glanced at the screen, which showed only static.

Then he walked over to the ladder that led up to the hatch.

"We don't know what's out there," Iscia warned. "Goffman might be waiting for us."

"We don't have any choice," William replied. "It's not like we can stay down here."

William climbed the ladder. He grabbed the locking wheel and twisted as hard as he could. The round hatch opened with a loud click, and William pushed it up.

He cautiously stuck his head up and peeked out.

They were back in the reservoir.

Black smoke rose from half of the bus, still over by the entrance. The other half of the bus was lying upside down a little way away.

The solid iron beams in the ceiling were deformed and glowed red like coals. Damaged power cables crackled. William shuddered. He turned around and looked down at Iscia, who was right below him.

"It looks like the water is electrified," he said. "And it's a complete mess up here. But I don't see anyone else."

"That doesn't necessarily mean we're the only ones here," Iscia said.

"I'll go first and check," William said. "And then you come after me with the orbulator."

"Okay."

He grabbed the handle. Time to get going. They had to get out of there. And the door by the bus was the only exit.

William clenched his teeth and climbed through the hatch. The smell of burning rubber hit him.

39

William let go of the ladder on the outside of the submarine and stepped onto the edge of the concrete pier.

Iscia followed his progress from the hatch up on top. William turned around to survey the reservoir. The massive iron exit door was only ten yards away, and it was ajar. For all he knew, danger could be waiting for them in the corridor beyond it. He had to check before he could signal to Iscia that it was safe to come down with the orbulator. They couldn't take any chances now that they had the antiluridium. Cautiously he moved toward the door. He carefully stepped over the downed power cables that lay sparking on the wet concrete floor.

William looked at the smoldering wreckage of the bus partially blocking the entrance. The heat radiated at him, and his face was hot. He took off his jacket, wadded it up, and held it in front of his face. It was so hot it felt like his hair might catch fire. He mostly wanted to run to the open doorway and keep going out into the cool, dark corridor beyond. But he didn't know what was out there. He had to be careful.

William stopped at the door. The heat from the bus wreckage was almost unbearable.

"William!" he heard Iscia yell, but he had to focus. Without turning around he raised his hand and gestured for her to wait.

He leaned forward and peeked out into the corridor. It was long and dark. A few old lightbulbs gave off enough light that William could see there was no one there. It would have to do. They needed to get out. And up.

"William!" It was Iscia again.

"There's no one here." William turned around. "We need to get—" He stiffened when he saw who had joined them.

Goffman stood motionless, staring at William with crazy eyes. The same unpredictable roaming gaze that Cornelia Strangler had had. Something had changed in his face. He was more Cornelia than Goffman now. And most of all, his face was aglow with lunacy. Big sections of his hair had been singed off. One whole side of his face was covered with an enormous burn. The fingers on his mechanical hand moved restlessly back and forth.

William didn't know what to do. Iscia was trapped in the submarine. If she came ashore, Goffman would get his claws on her and the orbulator. If she jumped into the water, she would be cooked by the live electrical wires.

"Where is it?" It was no longer Goffman's voice, but rather Cornelia's.

"We don't have it with us." The words tumbled out of his mouth.

"Rubbish!" Goffman yelled. "You passed the test. Otherwise you wouldn't have come back. Where's the antiluridium?"

William's eyes were drawn back up to Iscia again, but he regretted it right away. He didn't want to shift Goffman's attention away from himself. As long as he kept Goffman talking, Iscia had time to think of some way to save them.

"Does she have it?" Goffman asked, staring at Iscia with his crazy eyes.

Before William could say anything, Iscia raised the orbulator and held it over the edge.

"Should I let go of it, William?" Iscia asked. "That'll at least stop him from getting it for a while."

William looked down into the dark water. He knew that if she dropped the orbulator, two things would happen. First it would be fried by thousands of volts, and then it would continue on down into the murky depths. He remembered what Phil had said. No one knew how deep this water actually went. It would take forever to get it back again.

"Wait," William said, staring at Goffman.

There had to be a way to talk some sense into him. William was sure that the old Goffman was in there somewhere, behind those freaky eyes and all the craziness.

"What happened to you, Goffman?" William asked. "Did Cornelia's hand do this to you?"

"Goffman has only himself to thank for this. That fool just couldn't leave the hand alone."

"Huh?" William said. Now Goffman was talking about himself in the third person, the way he'd done back at the Institute.

"Goffman isn't here anymore." Goffman's face sneered.

"What do you mean? I can see that it's you."

"This is just his body. He's not home in here anymore. There wasn't room for us both. I won. And now it's just me."

"And who are you?" William asked, even though he already knew the answer. A part of him wanted to cry. Goffman was gone, and they might never get him back again.

"You know full well who I am."

"Cornelia." The name left a bad taste in William's mouth, as if he could taste that burned smell that always followed her.

Goffman smiled. Or, well, apparently it wasn't Goffman anymore. It was Cornelia, William's worst nightmare. She was back.

"Goffman realized he had made a terrible mistake the first time he tried the hand," Cornelia continued. "But by then it was too late. The hand had already transferred me to him. And there wasn't any way for him to get rid of me. Slowly but surely I took control of his body."

Cornelia paused and trained those crazy eyes on William, as if she really wanted him to understand what she was telling him. She was going to win them over.

"He resisted me as best he could, tried to save all his precious robots, retired them and hid them up in the attic. He had an intentional falling out with Benjamin so he would quit and leave the Institute. He probably didn't want Benjamin to see him transform into me."

Cornelia looked up at Iscia, as if to make sure she was still there. Then her dark eyes returned to William.

"Then the Orbulator Agent suddenly appeared," she continued, sneering. "Goffman knew I would do everything in my power to get the orbulator and to destroy it."

"Were you inside the hand when he touched it the first time?" William asked quietly.

"Of course," Cornelia said. "After the incident at the Crypto Portal, it was the only way I could get away. I defragmented myself and stored myself in the hand. I knew it would only be a question of time before someone put it on. And then I would be free again, like a genie in a bottle."

Cornelia grinned nastily. "But it was a big surprise that Goffman was the one who put it on. He just wanted to try it on, poor man. What a huge mistake!"

"Where is Goffman now?" William could hardly bear to listen to the answer.

"He's gone for good," Cornelia responded.

"But . . . ," William began.

"Enough chitchat," Cornelia said, and turned toward the submarine. William looked up.

"Where is she?" Cornelia's hoarse voice shook.

"Here!" Iscia popped up from the hatch again.

"Give me the orbulator," Cornelia demanded. Without looking at William, she pointed her mechanical hand right at him. "Or I'll pulverize him."

William could see that Iscia was planning something. She was staring down into the dark water. William followed her gaze but saw only darkness.

"Give it to me!" Cornelia's piercing voice reverberated through the massive space like an echo.

Now William spotted something down in the water, a small fleck of light. The fleck was coming closer, growing and becoming larger.

"Catch." Iscia tossed what she was holding in her hands down to Cornelia.

Cornelia ran toward the submarine with both hands out-stretched. She stopped right at the water's edge and actually managed to catch what Iscia had thrown.

Cornelia was holding the old radio in her hands, the same radio that William had used to summon Emma.

"A radio?" Cornelia asked, looking to Iscia. "Why did you give me a radio?"

Her face contorted with rage. She aimed her mechanical hand at Iscia and, with a loud zap, fired off a beam. Iscia ducked, and the beam flew past the submarine and exploded against the ceiling.

"I'm going to—" Cornelia began to shriek, but she didn't have a chance to finish before a colossal tentacle shot up out of the water and grabbed her. It lifted her high into the air. Cornelia screamed and dropped the radio. A tremendous cloud of sparks shot into the air as the radio hit the water.

The tentacle vanished into the depths, taking Cornelia with it. She screamed as her body hit the electrified water. She twitched and cramped violently before going limp. The tentacle let go and slid silently into the water.

William and Iscia stood there in shock and looked at the lifeless body.

William's legs were trembling, and Iscia was already climbing down the ladder on the outside of the submarine.

Once she was down, she turned to William.

"You think he—or she—is dead?" she whispered.

"Yes," William said solemnly.

He knew that it was actually Cornelia Strangler who lay in front of them. She had taken over Goffman's body, and they had paid the ultimate price. Now they were both gone.

40

William and Iscia were standing outside Big Ben. The door behind them in the clock tower wall shrank and disappeared.

The pyramid was hidden inside William's sweater. The place was crawling with cars and busy people. None of them seemed to notice William or Iscia.

He looked up at the clock face at the top of the tower.

"It's running again." He smiled.

Iscia didn't seem to care about the clock right now. She was staring at something in front of them.

"Who's that over there?" She pointed into the crowd.

William spotted a man in a baseball cap and a puffy blue jacket. The cap cast a shadow over his face, but he seemed to be staring in their direction. It was impossible to tell who he was.

"Come on." William pulled Iscia along behind him. "Someone has noticed us."

They climbed over the fence and fought their way through the throng of people. William turned to see if the man was following them but couldn't see him. William hoped he was just a completely normal tourist who'd happened to notice two kids inside the security fence.

At any rate, they needed to find a safe place where they could plan how to get back to the Institute with the orbulator.

They kept fighting their way through the crowd, and a few minutes later they were standing beside a large statue of Winston Churchill. There were fewer people here, and they were able to heave a sigh of relief. Sweat was pouring down William's face. It was hard work clearing a path like that while also safeguarding a heavy metal pyramid.

"He's still after us." Iscia nodded back in the direction they'd come from.

The man was coming straight at them, and there was no longer any doubt that they were being pursued.

"Who could it be?" Iscia asked.

"Dunno. Maybe a totally normal tourist? But we can't take any chances now since we have the antiluridium with us."

They ran across the street.

"There!" Iscia pointed to a line of trees at the end of the street.

They were running as fast as they could now.

William glanced back as he ran. The man was still after them and moving fast.

William and Iscia continued right out into the roadway, and a car honked and had to swerve to avoid hitting them. They jumped over a low wrought-iron fence into a green park and ran down one of the paved footpaths. They were heading for a large lake where two white swans were dozing.

"In there!" Iscia declared.

Soon they were surrounded by tall trees and dense shrubbery. The vegetation filtered away the noise of the city. All they could hear now was a distant hum.

"Up here." William gabbed a branch on a big tree and started climbing.

The bark had been worn away by the thousands of hands of the children who'd climbed and played here before them. But William and Iscia weren't here to play. They were here to hide. They climbed higher, in among the branches.

Soon they were sitting in the middle of all the foliage, trying to hide behind the branches, for the second time in a short while.

William startled when he heard a sound behind him. A little squirrel hopped along the branch they were sitting on and then jumped over to a nearby branch. It settled down there and started gnawing on a large nut while watching them curiously.

"Do you think he'll find us?" Iscia whispered.

William looked down at the ground. He had a hunch that whoever was following them wouldn't give up that easily.

The dense bushes rustled, and the man came into view. He continued toward their tree and stopped right below it. It was as if he knew they were there.

William held his breath. He thought about all they'd been through in the last few days. He couldn't let anyone take the pyramid away from him now, not after everything he'd done to get it.

William looked over at the squirrel, which seemed to have lost its appetite. The squirrel appeared to look back at William, as if checking his reaction, before it dropped the nut it was holding right over the man below.

Now it was as if William experienced everything in slow motion. The nut fell slowly toward the man. For a moment, William thought the nut was going to miss him, but no. It grazed one of the branches, changed course, and hit the man's cap.

The man tilted his head back and looked up. Soon he would discover them. Suddenly it was as if William was operating on autopilot. He pulled the pyramid out of his sweater and gave it to Iscia. Then he jumped off the branch he was sitting on, aiming for the man below.

The man tried to move out of the way, but it was too late.

William hit him full force, and they both fell to the ground.

William stayed on him. He had to hold the man down so Iscia could get away with the orbulator.

"Run, Iscia," he yelled. "Run!"

He heard Iscia climbing down out of the tree. And he heard her land beside him.

"William" he suddenly heard from underneath him. "Get off of me!" William looked down. Why did the man talk like a robot?

William sat up. "You know who I am?"

"Of course," the man replied. "Maybe you could let me stand up?"

William removed the man's cap and gasped when he saw who was hidden beneath it.

A robot lay there looking up at him with glowing eyes. William recognized it right away. It was the robot Goffman had taken from Benjamin, the crypto-bot he was going to use to solve the pyramid, the one Benjamin had loaded William's grandfather into.

William didn't budge. He wasn't planning on letting the robot go yet.

"Why are you following us?" he asked.

"It's me," the crypto-bot said. "Grandpa."

41

William was seated between his grandfather—his robot grandfather—and Iscia on the top deck of a red, double-decker London bus. It felt strange to sit on a bus like this after what had happened in the underground reservoir. On some level, William thought he could still feel the heat from that smoldering bus wreckage.

He was having a hard time taking his eyes off his grandfather.

"Someone will pick up Goffman's body and clean up the place," Grandfather said. "He deserves a proper funeral."

William nodded. They sat in silence for a little while longer.

"It's a little strange that you can walk around without anyone reacting," Iscia finally said.

"This is London," William's robot grandfather said. "It takes more than this to make people react."

William glanced down at the pyramid, which was once again safely tucked inside his sweater. "We have to get this back to the Institute as quickly as we can," he said.

Grandpa seemed like he wanted to say something but wasn't sure how to express it.

"I have some bad news." He watched William's face.

"What?"

"About the Institute."

"Yes?" William waited anxiously for him to continue.

"We can't go back there," Grandpa said. "The place is in ruins. The Institute was destroyed in the battle between the new and old robots. And Goffman—I mean Cornelia—made sure to raze what was left before she set off in pursuit of you two."

They were silent for a moment. William stared blankly into space. He couldn't believe it. Was the Institute really gone?

"We've decided to team up with the Center for Misinformation. Benjamin has taken over as director and decided to move everything to a secret location," Grandpa continued. "Go underground."

"But then what will we do?" William looked down at his sweater. "The orbulator needs to be somewhere safe."

"I know," Grandpa said, pushing the stop button. "That's precisely why we're here."

A moment later they were standing on the sidewalk watching the bus drive away.

"Come on." Grandpa started walking.

"Where are we going?" William asked.

"To a secure location. You've been there before."

"I have?" William looked at Iscia, who merely shrugged.

Grandpa turned off the busy main street down a narrow side street. There wasn't a soul in there, and it smelled of rotten food. The street was full of trash cans and rubbish that people had discarded.

Grandpa looked around before ducking behind a big green shipping container. William and Iscia followed. Grandpa stopped in front of a round manhole cover.

"Keep a lookout." He squatted down. "Tell me if anyone's coming."

He pulled an old key out of his jacket pocket, ran his metallic fingers over the pattern on the manhole cover, and stopped by something that at first glance looked like a crack.

Grandpa inserted the key into the crack and turned it. A faint click came from inside the manhole cover. Grandpa stood up and took a couple of steps back.

With a jerk, the manhole cover disappeared, pulled down into the darkness with a screechy scraping sound. The scraping faded away and was replaced by a distant hum.

The hum grew louder, and a shiny metal tube rose out of

the hole. Grandpa stepped up to the tube and entered a code into a control panel. A door opened with a metallic swish.

"Come on." Grandpa stepped into the tube.

"After you." William nodded to Iscia.

She disappeared into the tube. Once William had also squeezed in, the door slid shut, and they whizzed downward at tremendous speed.

William felt the tube turning back and forth and up and down. It was like riding a roller coaster, only much faster.

They jerked to a stop. The door slid open, and bright light flooded in.

Grandpa got out with William and Iscia right behind him.

William looked around. They were in a large room. The tube they had just stepped out of was sticking up out of the floor behind them.

"Welcome," said a merry woman's voice.

A large, plump woman was approaching them on a sort of golf cart mounted atop a hovering air cushion. She was wearing dark sunglasses. Two wires ran from either side of her glasses and into her head. William recognized her immediately. His grandfather was right. He had been here before.

The woman driving toward them was Professor Wellcrow. She was the head of the Center for Misinformation. This was where William, Goffman, and Benjamin had hidden when they went down into the secret tunnels deep beneath Victoria Station to look for Grandpa. It felt like such an incredibly long time ago now. So much had happened since then.

The hovercraft stopped right in front of them. Professor Wellcrow was grinning broadly.

"Do you have it?" she asked. "The orbulator?"

William looked at his grandfather, who nodded to him.

"I have it here." William pointed to his sweater.

"Perfect." Wellcrow clapped her hands together in satisfaction. "Put it in there." She pointed to something that looked like a safe that came wheeling over to William.

The safe stopped right in front of him, and a hatch opened on its top.

"It'll be safe in there," the professor said.

William pulled the orbulator out from under his sweater and looked at it. It felt strange to hand it over after all he'd been through.

"You'll get it back soon enough," Grandpa said. "After all, you're the only one who can use it."

William walked over to the safe and carefully placed the orbulator down in it. The lid closed, and the safe drove off.

Suddenly William felt a tremendous sense of relief at being rid of the orbulator. It was as if he had gotten rid of all the other things that had happened as well.

"We'll take good care of it." Professor Wellcrow smiled.

"If there's anything we're good at here at the Center for Misinformation, it's keeping things secret."

William nodded and looked over at Iscia. She smiled at him. Her eyes beamed in triumph.

"William," a familiar voice suddenly said.

Benjamin came striding toward him on those long legs of his. And before William could say anything at all, Benjamin had caught him up in a gigantic bear hug.

"I was actually a little afraid I wouldn't get to see you two again," he said, setting William back down. He proceeded over to Iscia and gave her a hug too.

Once the hugging was done, Benjamin gave them a serious look.

"You heard what happened to the Institute, then?" he asked.

"I told them," Grandpa said.

"And you know that we've gone underground and that the Institute for Post-Human Research is going to join forces with the Center for Misinformation?"

William and Iscia nodded.

"It's going to be great," Benjamin said, and looked over at Professor Wellcrow, who smiled and clapped her hands together, and the sound reverberated through the room.

42

William closed the door to his room and walked over to his newly installed desk.

They had returned home from London the day before, and the work of setting up the furniture that was being delivered in flat boxes was still underway.

"Dinner!" his mother called from the kitchen downstairs.

"Coming!" William replied, and sat down on his new chair. He just had to take *one* last peek at what was in the drawer.

The new desk wasn't as big as the old one, but it had several drawers. And William liked that. He looked into one of them.

It was still there, the box that Benjamin had given him right before they left the Center for Misinformation. It was brushed metal and the size of a shoe box. There were nine glowing buttons on the lid with numbers on them.

William lifted the box out of the drawer and set it on the desk in front of him. He entered the combination, and the lid flipped open with a brief blip.

William took out what was inside and sat gazing at what he now held in his hands.

An orb.

His own orb.

The orb he'd received the first time he went to the Institute for Post-Human Research.

William ran his fingers over all the symbols on its surface.

"The food's getting cold," his mother called from the kitchen.

William put the orb back in the box and flipped the lid shut again. It felt comforting to know that it was in his desk drawer in his room.

William went downstairs and stopped when he saw his father sprawled on the floor in the middle of the living room. He was scratching his head while moving around the parts that would eventually become a bookshelf.

"Are you still at it?" a robot voice asked from somewhere else in the room.

Robot Grandpa entered the room. His big robot body clanked against the wood floor. He was wearing mechanics' coveralls and holding a toolbox in one hand. He stopped beside William's father and set the toolbox down.

William's father didn't answer him. He scratched his head some more and moved the parts around.

"I finished all the upstairs cupboards," Grandpa said. "What if you unscrew that piece there and then screw it in over there?"

"No." William's father gave Grandpa a look of exasperation. "I already tried that. That's not it."

William could tell that his father was trying to sound gruff. But even though his father hadn't come right out and told Grandpa so, William knew he was overjoyed to have him back.

"DINNER!" William's mother yelled again.

"Okay . . . okay!" William's father tossed the instructions aside.

He stood up and headed for the kitchen. Grandpa remained, looking at all the pieces on the floor.

William's mother appeared in the kitchen doorway.

"William," she said, pointing with a spatula at him. "Time to eat. And the same goes for you." She pointed at Grandpa, too.

"I'm a robot," Grandpa said. "I don't need to eat."

"Well, you have to come sit with us anyway," William's mother said sternly. "Manners!"

Grandpa set down the screwdriver and clomped into the kitchen.

"Iscia!" William's mother called out.

"Coming!" Iscia replied, running into the living room. "Are you coming?" She smiled at William and then disappeared into the kitchen.

The Institute had been Iscia's home. And now that it had been destroyed, she basically had nowhere to live. She could have stayed at the Center for Misinformation, but William's parents had insisted that she come live with them.

William stopped in the kitchen doorway.

He stood there looking at his parents, his robot grandfather, and Iscia, all sitting around the table.

They seemed almost like a normal family.

Almost.